Archie Comes Home

Peter (

~ With best
wishes,

Peter Quince

ISBN: 978-1-326-24546-7

ACKNOWLEDGEMENTS

First of all my gratitude to David Morrison at PublishNation for encouraging the hatching of this book and convincing me that I could fly when I felt earthbound. Next, thanks to Pauline Hiam who transformed my fledgling text into something a publisher might nurture and coax into maturity. Scott Gaunt has done wonders with the cover design, capturing the story's essence. Most of all thanks to Jan, my wife, for helping me bring my story out of the dark and into the light of day when I had tucked it away dormant and neglected.

Oh. . . and thanks to owls everywhere!

CHAPTER ONE

A Wise Man

When Archie Edgar woke up in the morning, all he could hear was the sound of the television rising through his bedroom floor from downstairs. It was always the same. He tried to ignore it. Every morning he tried his best. Archie preferred the chatter of birds to the blether of human voices.

He peeped out of his bedroom window. Whiteness as far as the eye could see. It nearly blinded him. The snow was a gift, though not an unexpected one. He was so happy he took an enormous breath and felt his whole body glow, tingle, expand.

Snow at last! (In it the dark of a bird could be seen more easily.)

He knew it would come. It always came early in that part of Scotland where he lived, near the oil rigs. Supersonic crystals straight from Siberia.

His family had lived and worked there for longer than photographs had existed. So his Uncle Craig always said.

It wasn't even near to Christmas yet. Snow carried a tingly joy. But sadness shuffled close behind it. A row of angels with a devil in the rear.

Archie Edgar had only one friend – Rory, no second name – and there was no way that Rory could ever play in the snow with him. Rory just wasn't suited to snow. He wasn't built for it. He existed only in summer sunshine, in a kind of warm glow. And he was trapped.

Rory was a special friend in more ways than one, but he never spoke and he never played outside. He couldn't. And Archie hardly ever saw him. The way they communicated was special, too.

It was a strange life to find yourself in the middle of.

"Archie, come down and get yer breakfast and don't dawdle in yer bedroom!"

His father's voice shot right through the brickwork of the house, not to mention floors and ceilings. Mr Edgar – 'Dodie' to family and friends – ruled with an iron rod. He had to.

His wife Mollie – Archie's mother – wasn't usually up to handling breakfast, dinner, supper or anything else much. She hadn't been able to do so for at least a year.

Archie knew there was something wrong with her. He felt sorry for her, his own mother. So sorry at times that he felt like gathering up all her bottles – the green, the brown and the colourless – in a big bag and dragging them down to the tip where white gulls screamed and dive-bombed and snatched greedily at almost anything.

Mr Edgar was waiting in the kitchen. He only ever went there during breaks between television programmes, or very swiftly to raid the fridge when the ads were on. Mr Edgar lived on the sofa.

"Late again, Arch!"

"But it's only nine, Dad, and there's snow. . ."

"Horrible stuff!"

"But it's great to play in."

"You best stay in. Catch a death out there. And I canna afford medicine. Wind's coming off the North Sea, straight through the old rigs. You can be sure o' that. There, gobble up yer Krispies."

Archie dropped his head. He didn't want his father to catch the sour expression on his face. He sat at one end of the table and looked down into the bowl of Krispies. All he saw was the pure white of the milk dirtied by flecks of pale brown. It didn't look like food at all. (A dark quick bird flashed across his mind.)

Mr Edgar said, "And when you've finished, lad, come and curl up on the sofa wi' me. Good film's on telly. Too cold to go messin' about out there."

Archie knew where his mother would be. She had a room of her own that no one else was allowed into, except in emergencies. It was at the back of the house. It was a room that looked out onto a tiny garden, but the curtains were always closed like a shut eye, a bruised one.

Sometimes she appeared unexpectedly, and she smiled a lot. But in her smile Archie saw something that had fallen down, as if a bright bird had flown out of her and never returned.

He knew he had to accept the situation. He had no brothers and sisters to fall back on. The one sister he'd had no longer existed. Archie could hardly even remember her. But he knew his mother could, all too clearly. All too often.

Rosie arrived in winter too. The last winter a year ago. She didn't stay very long. Archie recalled seeing her once when she came out of hospital. Then she went straight back that same night. There was snow everywhere that day. Rosie's tiny face was just as pale as the snow, Archie remembered. When Archie quietly asked his mother where Rosie had gone, all he saw was a wet mask instead of a real face.

Things were different now. Better in some ways, much worse in others.

It was Friday again. And every Friday Archie went to stay overnight with his Uncle Craig and his Aunty Brenda. They lived in the lodge – the old granite forrester's cottage – near Hirn. It was on the Aberdeen side of Midmar Forest, about ten miles from the city. West, that is. If you went ten miles east you skimmed the North Sea and the oil rigs.

Friday was Archie's favourite day, had been for years. He loved being on 'loan' to his favourite uncle and aunt. They'd never had any children of their own – not even a lost baby.

The arrangement was the same every week; Uncle Craig drove into Aberdeen and headed for Torry, a maze of streets near Nigg Bay. He sat down, had a cup of tea, ignored the chattering television (which Dodie Edgar never seemed to switch off), asked how Mollie was, and carried Archie's rucksack to the Land Rover. All this time Aunty Brenda kept the lodge warm with seasoned logs from the forest and prepared a home-made fish supper.

Archie felt his heartbeat quicken with excitement whenever Friday came around. He wanted to be inside Midmar Forest more than almost anything except seeing his mother well again and praying that Rosie might return by some miracle.

3

Archie felt that if anyone could bring Rosie back, his Uncle Craig could. That man could do anything. He was what Miss Lewis at school called a 'wise man', a man who might easily have stepped right out of a bible story.

'Wise man' sounded similar to 'wise owl', which was another thing to think about.

Uncle Craig held Archie's rucksack in one hand and put his other hand across Archie's shoulders and said to Dodie, "We'll be off, then."

"See you tomorrow afternoon, Dad."

Archie yearned for his father to turn and get up and kiss him good bye, but all he said was, "Yeah, okay, tomorrow after footba'." He never once took his eyes off the television. It was as if he didn't really care.

The fish supper was on the table when Uncle Craig opened the porch door of the lodge and let Archie slip in before him. It was steaming. The whole room smelled like a chip shop.

As always, Aunty Brenda ran over to Archie and hugged him so tightly he felt his innards rise up to his throat.

"Here, let me take off yer coat and scarf." She was overjoyed.

Hirn Lodge was always so warm.

It made Archie feel guilty; he couldn't help it.

In some ways he'd rather his mother made him a fish supper. She used to, before Rosie. But you couldn't fry fish in the backroom.

Uncle Craig bent down before the crackling log fire and pushed the palms of his hands towards the dancing flames and then rubbed them together.

"Cold enough, Bren?"

"Aye. When isn't it?"

Archie sat at the small table in the tiny room. Everything about the granite cottage was on a miniature scale, cosy and welcoming and unlike anything back in the city.

He gobbled down the fish supper rapidly and in silence. He loved to hear his aunt and uncle chatter, one each side of the fireplace snuggled in identical armchairs. He wished the world could always

4

be like this, always a Friday evening in Midmar Forest surrounded by the smell of home-cooked food.

But all things change. They changed a year ago when Rosie came and went. It was all so sudden. Like a circus arriving when the big top lights up and everyone cheers and then there's a massive power cut and everyone goes silent and it seems like there never was a circus in the first place.

Archie had only a few thick-cut chips left on his plate when he remembered something. He turned towards the fireplace.

"Uncle Craig?"

"Yes little'un?"

"You haven't forgotten about the owl, have you?"

Uncle Craig looked puzzled. "Owl? Now what owl would that be?"

Aunty Brenda always saw something playful in Uncle Craig's expression. A half-hidden smile appeared on her face. She looked across at Archie. He sat like a statue with his fork in the air and a single chip stuck on its prongs. The penny dropped. He couldn't help but break into a smile himself.

A joker to the end, that was his uncle. Never a straight answer. 'Owl, what owl?' As if he didn't know.

Uncle Craig said, "Now don't choke on your last chip. We'll talk in the morning about feathery creatures. I might have a little surprise for you."

The core of Archie's body glowed as brightly as the flames which danced back and forth along the top of a log. There was magic in that living fireplace. There was magic in the forest. In Uncle Craig's heart there was a kind of magic too, if magic is to do with what's good in the world.

What's possible after all the hurt?

CHAPTER TWO

Five Beauties

Uncle Craig insisted on whispering. "Look there, little'un, between those conifers."

He pointed.

Archie could see nothing but bracken dotted with a thin powdery layer of snow. Midmar Forest rose high above the two crouching figures.

"Where? I can't see much."

Uncle Craig pretended to be cross. "Well, open your eyes wider."

Archie tried to open his eyes wider.

"All I can see is snow and trees."

"I told you, you're not looking sharply enough."

Archie began to panic. He wondered whether his eyesight was poor. Had all that snow half blinded him? Uncle Craig must have eagle eyes.

He felt a little tug on his coat sleeve. "Come on, I'll show you, give you a close-up."

Uncle Craig took Archie to the base of a conifer. He pointed down at their feet. "There," he said. Archie stared. What he saw was a mass of interwoven twigs, untidy and flattened out and embroidered with snow. It wasn't much. There were odd bits and pieces surrounding the twigs. Bits like pellets and pieces like bone.

Archie looked up at his uncle, as puzzled as before. "What is it?"

"What is it?" echoed Uncle Craig, as if he couldn't believe that Archie didn't know. And then he squatted down slowly and tugged at Archie's sleeve again so that Archie bent low with him. The mass of untidy twigs lay between them, framed by their knees.

"It's an old nest."

"Nest?"

6

"Yes. Look. Study it, Little'un. You must observe all things slowly and closely. Or they vanish. Secret of life. One of them, at least."

Archie thought his uncle sounded like a teacher. Sometimes he did. Archie wasn't keen on teachers, but made an exception in this case. He said, "I can see it now, Uncle, but it doesn't look much."

"Not now. But back in March there were five pure white eggs in there. Five beauties. I kept them a secret. Came out every day to sit and watch. Took a long time. But then I saw the eggs move all by themselves. And then little cracks appeared in one of them. And then – what do you think?"

Archie kept staring at the flattened, snow-dappled mass of twigs. He couldn't believe it had once been a nest, couldn't believe there had been warm eggs in that spot which moved by themselves until life popped out.

With a dreamy sense of wonder, Archie whispered, "Owls?"

He looked up at Uncle Craig, who smiled broadly. Uncle Craig nodded. "Owlets. Five beauties."

"But what about the mother?"

"Oh, she came back and forth constantly. My presence didn't seem to bother her that much. She barked at me once or twice."

Archie gave his uncle a puzzled look. "Barked? That's what dogs do."

"And long-eared owls. Marks them out from any other kind. A funny sort of barking cry, broken up by a lot of yap-yap-yaps. You'd know it if you heard it. And you'd never forget it."

Archie was amazed.

In the middle of the forest, surrounded by snow-flecked tree trunks, he studied the owl's nest. He wanted to see pure white eggs. He wanted to see owlets struggling from shells. He wanted to hear the mother's bark. He wanted to see what was no longer there.

Archie whispered, "Five eggs. And now there are five owls and they're gone."

"All but one."

Archie turned his gaze from the nest to his uncle, whose smile had the devil in it, as Dodie Edgar always said about his own son's.

"One?"

"Just the one."

"What do you mean, Uncle Craig?"

"I can't tell you, but I'll show you." He tapped the side of his nose. "Later."

"No, now!" Archie felt the sharp edge of his own voice. He felt that his uncle was teasing him, deliberately spinning a mystery. Which he was. It builds excitement and makes the surprise much bigger. But it's maddening.

The two walked back through the forest, Uncle Craig with his hand on Archie's shoulder. Everything felt clean and pure. It was so different to Aberdeen. The city seemed closed and cramped and dark. Only the sea, fanning out to the east, meant freedom, and Midmar Forest was an ocean of trees.

Uncle Craig insisted that it had to be 'Later'. Too much excitement in one day was not good for any boy. (Archie kept seeing flashing images of owls with tufted ears barking like dogs.)

Saturday morning. Soon Uncle Craig would get out the Land Rover and trundle him back to Aberdeen, stopping just short of the coast-line. As always, Archie had confused feelings: he didn't want to leave his uncle's hidden cottage, and yet he yearned to reach home and find his mother bright and cheerful and cooking his favourite meals again. It never happened. One day, he thought.

Archie lay on the bed in the tiny room he was allowed to call his own on Fridays and Saturdays. He fumbled in his rucksack and found the notepad which had an elasticated clasp and a pencil shoved down the side in a pocket all its own. He never showed the notepad to a soul, not even his favourite aunt and uncle. He daren't.

He wrote:

Dear Rory,

I hope you are well. Also I hope to see you One Day. (Im always saying that!) Itll happen, Im sure. Things at home have to be sorted out first. Theres a lot of troble. Sometimes I put my ear aginst the wall of the backroom and I hear Number One mumbling a lot and the only word I can make out is Rosie becos that word comes out lowder than the rest. Sometimes I hear the clinkin of bottles and I want to run in there and grab them, even full ones, and run out to the dump and smash them in the skips. But I darnt. Number Two would do what hes done befor to me. Thats the only time Id rather be at school. Slooth came nocking at the door the other day and Number Two had to anser it. He said I was away at my uncles house and yes hed tell me and hed get me into schol even if he had to drag me hiself. Corse I didn't belive a word of it and nor did Slooth and I can tell that you dont ether.

Id better start a new pargraf. Ace came and picked me up as usal and drove me out to Camp. He took me deep into the Dreemplace and showed me something on the ground that didnt look anything much. He said 5 eggs had been there, then 5 babys, and theyd all lived and flone. He wouldnt tell me anymore. Ace likes misterys. So do I. But hes a teese as well. I felt very warm inside when he told me that all 5 babys had servived.

Things at home dont seem to change much. One day (see, Ive said it again!). I promise Ill try not to keep saying that. When we meet up Ill bite my tong if the words One day come anywere near my lips. It doesnt really matter tho does it?

Im getting the hang of paragrafs, see?

Ace has something up his sleeve. Ive got an idea what it is. But I cant tell you now just in case Im wrong. Then Ill really be down in the dumps.

Rory, we get so much snow up here, but every time it falls it seems like another wee bit of magic. I looked out my window the other morning and saw all the big flakes fluttering down slowly and I thought evry one of them is the sole of a child that died. Rosie must be among them somewere. Were else could she be?

I wanted to tell Number One of my idea but when I got to the door of the backroom I heard really lowd snoring. And I thought maybe its better shes asleep than awake. She always said to me Sweet dreams and that made the pillow feel a lot softer under my head. Corse, she doesnt say that now.

Ive gabbled on too long, Rory, (as usual). Hope to see you in the summer when your releesed. Until then I have to live here in the middle of Ploot. At least once a week I get taken to Camp in the Dreamplace, get it? Ive got a feather to give you. It flotes really slowly down from my bedroom cieling to the floor. It belonged to something majical. Something that lives were you are, kind of. Were I want to be.

Thats all for now.

Your frend, Archie

CHAPTER THREE

Wing-beating

Sometimes Dodie Edgar went into Mollie's room and he stayed there awhile. Sometimes it remained suspiciously quiet. Sometimes Archie stood with his ear against the wall and made it into a giant loud-speaker. Then he could hear their chatter, their raised voices, even their whispered words and his mother's jumping sobs. Sometimes his heart seemed to rise up through his chest and stand on end and whirl around, making him breathless. At such times he came very close to wishing he were back at school.

When his dad's eyes were glued to a good programme, Archie slipped down the passage and out the front door and closed it silently with a twist of the key. He knew now how to move like a draught that human ears couldn't pick up.

He stood at the desk of the Children's Library. No one seemed to pay him any attention. During schooldays this part of the library was almost dead. Sometimes mothers came in with screaming toddlers, but they turned round and went straight out again.

The library assistants were very busy. Too busy to notice Archie. He stood a long time watching, waiting. It was better than being at home but not as good as the forest, the lodge, the place where the flattened nest had been.

At last a young woman with glasses on the end of her nose approached him. "Can I help you?"

Archie stared into her face, terrified. Instantly the right words, the ones he'd practised and practised, slipped away from him.

The woman repeated, "Can I help you?"

Archie blurted out, "Owls."

"Pardon?"

"Have you got any books on them?"

The woman smiled sweetly. It came across far better than his own mother's smile. Like sunshine minus the clouds. "Shouldn't you be at school right now?"

"I'm ill."

"Ill?"

"Toothache."

"Oh." The woman leaned close over the counter. "Shouldn't you be at the dentist's, then?"

Archie looked all around the library, as if he needed an escape route. But then he heard the woman's voice, kinder now, as if she'd given in. "Come on, I'll show you the right section."

He breathed a sigh of relief and followed her.

The chair he sank into was painted bright blue and pink and yellow and was piled with plump cushions. There was nothing like it at home.

He ran his finger along the lines of print as he read:

"Long-eared owl: three to six dead white eggs are laid in March, April or May." The word 'dead' sent a shiver through him. It soon went. He looked up from the print. There wasn't a soul besides himself in the Children's Library. For once Archie felt relaxed.

He carried on running his finger over the words: "Makes a home in old crows' nests, but occasionally on the ground." (The word 'occasionally' gave him a bit of trouble.) "Feeds on mice, rats, moles, voles and other small rodents and sometimes small birds and insects." He recalled his Uncle Craig saying months ago that he needed to pay a visit to the hardware store in Aberdeen because it sold rat-traps. It all came back to him, fitted in. It was like a puzzle with many missing pieces, but some were falling into place.

Archie heard loud bleeps from a computer on a desk. The young woman with the glasses on the end of her nose was staring at the screen. Her fingers were dancing over the keyboard. It reminded him of Ms Lewis playing the piano in assembly. All around her there was a glow.

He began to feel slightly panicky, imagining that his father had dragged his eyes away from the television and gone upstairs and found his son's bedroom abandoned. And come across his little note-book with the elasticated clasp. Then there'd be more stick.

Archie skimmed the rest of the page, his index finger now hitting top speed: "Lives in forests and woodlands. . . the Long-Eared Owl is known for its peculiar barking cry, broken by dog-like 'yaps'. . . ears are really tufts of feathers, long and brown. . . overall buff plumage. . ." (What is 'buff'? he thought. 'Plumage' must mean its feathery coat) ". . The basic colour having brown streaks underneath with grey and brown spots on the back. . . before evening flight this bird indulges in a bout of beak-snapping and wing-beating."

That was it.

He'd understood all but a few strange words.

Archie closed his eyes and tried to picture a long-eared owl on the strength of this description. Nothing came clear and sharp. What he saw was a dim outline. Words alone couldn't bring alive the real thing. Books were not nests or forests or the wind in your hair.

He snapped the book shut and dropped it in the book-bin and smiled at the bespectacled lady on the way out. Then he ran all the way home.

He hadn't been missed.

His father called him into the lounge. Archie saw his dad sprawled full-length on the three-seat sofa, his usual place. In one hand he had a packet of crisps, in the other the remote. He was rapidly flicking through channels. Nothing he saw seemed to please him. Archie stared at the screen; it seemed to put him into a trance.

Mr Edgar squeezed himself onto one end of the sofa and patted the cushion. "Come on, Arch, shove up next to me. Cracking film on. Can't be missed."

Whenever Archie looked at his father, a strange feeling came over him, one he could hardly explain. He didn't want to explain it.

"Okay, Dad."

Archie sat down primly at one end of the sofa, bolt upright. His father grabbed him, almost in a rugby tackle, and pulled him into a tight bear hug and laughed deafeningly. "Tha's ma boy! Come and cuddle up wi' yer daddy!"

That strange feeling swept through him. It was like a sickness. It was like feeling guilty. It was like wishing you were elsewhere. It was like nothing on earth.

Archie felt suffocated.

"Film's about to start, just after these adverts. Have a crisp. Go get yourself some squash, lemonade or something. No beer, mind."

"No, it's okay, Dad."

Archie nestled his head into his father's shoulder. As the curtains were still closed, the poor natural light meant that their faces lit from the television screen like lanterns. Archie caught the odour of his father's body. It was familiar but far from pleasant. Stale and sharp.

Whatever film had begun didn't register in Archie's mind. He was looking but not seeing.

Mr Edgar grinned like a naughty little boy. "Car chase in this one, Arch."

"Is there?"

"Aye. I read about it in the guide. I love car chases, don't you?"

"Aye." Archie heard himself reply but it meant nothing. His mind settled elsewhere, like a bird in flight coming to rest somewhere lovely. The scatter of twigs where the eggs had been. The scrawny little necks of the fledglings, their beaks straining for food. Droppings – pellets, Uncle Craig called them – and the picked-clean bones of rats, mice, voles and moles arranged at the base of the conifer. The mother's outline in moonlight, her ear-tufts poking up, snapping her beak and beating her wings furiously. The pictures in his mind went on and on.

Suddenly Archie fell sideways. It brought him back with a jolt to the sitting room. His father had leapt off the sofa.

"Adverts! Quick, let's put the kettle on for a brew!" And he was gone.

The adverts flashed across the screen in quick succession. Nothing that Archie saw made much sense to him. It was like removing himself from the scene, except that the soundtrack still battered him.

He grabbed the remote and punched his finger on the right place and the television died. It felt like a brave act.

Before his father returned, Archie had terrible thoughts. He couldn't help himself.

What if Uncle Craig was his real father? The simple wish did not point to the truth. He knew that. But it felt like it.

Dodie Edgar thundered back into the room. "What's the telly off for?"

CHAPTER FOUR

Almost Too Small to be Human

Archie put his ear to the wall of the backroom. His father had been in there ages. There were long silences. Then sudden bursts of chatter. Most words sounded muffled, but now and again he caught a few. It was like a jigsaw puzzle of spoken language with a few clues but lots of pieces missing. He felt so frustrated not understanding. He felt so bad eavesdropping. But what could he do when his father spent half his life in one room of the house and his mother lived in another and he, their own son, didn't know quite where to be?

The door to the backroom opened slightly. Archie was sure his father's hand had twisted the doorknob. Archie was about to dash up the stairs, but the door didn't open any wider. And now he could easily make out his father's parting words:

"Are you sure, Mollie, are you sure?. . . Okay, then you'd better get yersel' along to the doctor's and tell him what you've just told me and have the tests to see if it's true. – And ye'd better lay off the bottle, eh? It'll not do the chances any good. . . Archie? Oh, I'll tell him when the time's right."

By the time these last few words had left his father's throat, Archie was half way up the stairs.

It all comes back.

Archie is sitting at the kitchen table. Best behaviour. Mum coming out of hospital. Dad'll be back with her soon. With her and the 'new addition', as he calls it. Rosie. Named months ago. He has followed instructions and put the kettle on the gas and keeps it simmering. They'll want oodles of tea, they always do. Tea and talk and a new arrival.

When he sees Rosie's face for the first time he is shocked. It's so tiny, almost too small to be human. And full of creases like an old lady's. And her eyes are closed and she smells faintly of blankets.

But he loves her. He knows he loves her straight away, before she makes her first sounds, gurgling like a little stream. He loves her even when that white-as-snow face darkens to a slatey blue and his mother begins to frown and calls 'Dodie! Dodie!' and his father takes one look and rushes out to call an ambulance and Archie remembers the prayers that Miss Lewis taught him in school and says them now even though he doesn't have a clue what they mean.

It all comes flooding back.

His father orders him up to his bedroom even though Archie hasn't finished praying and doesn't want to go. He stares at Rosie's face as his father yanks him off his knees and ushers him backwards out the lounge door. He hears his mother cooing to Rosie as though the new-born really needs comforting, really needs telling that life is worth it.

That's the last he ever sees of her.

What did Ms Lewis tell them in class, the last time he attended school? 'Animals can heal sick human beings.' Those were her exact words. Archie's thoughts flew back. He pictured the classroom the moment after she'd said it. He must have been gawping with open mouth, because the next thing he heard was, 'Archie Edgar, pay attention and stop daydreaming!' And every single child in the class burst into laughter except Agnie Robson, who sat across the aisle from him. She just glowered at everyone. He didn't like her but at least she didn't laugh. At least she didn't try to make him out a fool.

'Animals can heal sick human beings in many ways, children. For instance, elderly people often live alone except for a pet dog or cat. If they stroke that dog or cat frequently – as most do – then it lowers their blood pressure. It's been proved in experiments. And if you can lower your blood pressure you might feel better and live longer. . .'

Miss Lewis's words replayed in Archie's head. Even the peculiar rise and fall of her voice was there. He wasn't daydreaming anyway. He was simply amazed to hear that animals can heal sick human beings.

At times like that school wasn't so bad. You came across surprising things. You learned at unexpected moments. You shared knowledge and the eyes of the whole class bulged in unison hearing a gripping story or a jaw-dropping fact. But if your dad didn't force you to go and your mother was always somewhere else, it was hard just to get out of bed on chilly mornings. People got into certain habits. Easy ones. Bad ones.

Archie thought: I can't stand you, Agnie Robson, but thank you for being the only one not to laugh. Then he felt guilty.

Uncle Craig always looked forward to Fridays, the same as Archie did. It was then he acquired a 'son' just for a short while. And the misty look on Aunty Brenda's face each time that Archie arrived was worth all the heartache of a house lacking children's laughter.

Uncle Craig walked from the lodge to the shed, as he did every morning. He had to if the long-eared owl was to remain his 'friend'. He liked to think of the bird this way, although he knew that a wild animal of any kind could never really be a friend. The wildness in it would always be there, making it ready to take off and re-join its own kind. Soon, he hoped, it would become Archie's 'friend'.

The rat traps caught enough rats and mice and moles and voles to keep the young owl in breakfast, lunch and super, not to mention snacks in between.

Uncle Craig had been training the owl ever since he'd found the nest at the base of a conifer – the one he'd taken Archie to – and whipped away just one of the fine warm eggs, way back in March. He remembered mumbling an apology to the mother owl for committing such a crime against nature. It was almost kidnapping. But he was determined to carry out his long-term highly secret plan for Archie's sake. The young lad would never believe it. And Uncle Craig knew that his nephew needed something outside his home to focus on, some amazing companion, something that would boost him and make a budding expert out of him. It would be ten times better than library books and a hundred times better than television.

He opened the shed door and let in early morning light.

The nine-months-old bird fluttered on its perch.

"Okay, okay, calm down. I'm here wi' your breakfast."

Uncle Craig lifted a transparent plastic bag which contained a jumble of fresh-killed rodents. He knew the bird would prefer live prey, catching its own, but that would be too difficult. Either the prey would escape or the owl would. Anyway, it was still young.

The long-eared owl cocked its head to one side. It made a soft cheeping sound, nothing like a bark. It flapped its wings for exercise and Uncle Craig felt a powerful draught. The bird was getting bigger and stronger every day.

"You've no name yet, owl. Little'un'll gie yer one, I'm sure. Leave it to him."

Uncle Craig tipped the bag up and the rodents fell out onto the dirt floor. The owl's head swivelled and it looked down. Its eyes were like radar scanners. Now it was almost fully trained.

Later that day Uncle Craig would take it out on a long leash and circle it around himself in a big clearing he called the Meadow. One day he would have to remove the restraint. And hope.

The bird flew like quicksilver. Archie would soon see magic of another kind. Something born in his imagination.

CHAPTER FIVE

Back to School

It looked like a big dark bird of prey ghosting clean through the backroom.

He stood at the foot of the stairs and stared at the tightly shut door along the hallway. A jagged shadow of the bird's wingtips rose and fell as it seemed to sweep right through the walls. A ghost-bird. A kind of moving darkness. A miserable thing darkening the whole back of the house. Where could it have gone?

So often, Archie stared at that tightly shut door. So often he stood and listened. If there wasn't silence it was only because he could hear the muffled music and juddery voices coming from the sitting room television. His father's roaring laughter and choking fits

On the odd occasion he tapped, very lightly, at the backroom door. As if it would bite him. Or suddenly open wide and terrify him not with his mother's face but that of an ugly beaked bird, like a gargoyle. It all arose from dreams. He lived in dreams, some wonderful, some shattering, some a helter-skelter mixture of both.

When the shadow of the huge bird had gone, Archie drummed his fingers on the out-of-bounds door. It set his heart skipping.

The door opened, just a little. His mother stood there smiling that bruised smile.

"Archie, love! Come in, come in!"

Mrs Edgar rarely asked him into her refuge. He thought she was ashamed. She put an arm across his shoulders. He felt himself shiver and a lump came into his throat. He couldn't say a word. It was a home inside a home, the centre of something he could rarely reach.

Archie sat beside his mother on her bed. She fluffed up his hair.

"You look so pale and peaky, Arch."

He looked up at her. "So do you, Mum."

She took him by the shoulders and made him stare into her eyes. She was almost fierce. "Archie, please try to understand."

He gave her a dumb look: he *was* trying.

She said, "Since Rosie. . . I'm trying, but it's so hard."

"I know, Mum. I want Rosie back, and I want you back."

She clutched his head against her shoulder. "Archie, Archie, you will have Rosie back, I promise you. Sort of."

He pulled his head away from her and studied her face hard. He was amazed. Was this the truth? The sister that he'd hardly seen for more than the blink of an eye?

"Don't look so surprised, Archie love. I promise you another Rosie. . . Now will you go back to school like a good boy?"

Archie couldn't take into his head the sudden shift from Rosie to school. He was confused. What made it worse – like the dark shadow of the huge bird returning – was when she asked him, "Wouldn't you rather live with your Aunty Brenda? It would only be for a while until. . . I know you love Fridays. I know you can't wait to go over there."

"But that's because. . ."

Archie found that the words wouldn't come. And the words wouldn't come because he didn't know what he did want. He loved Hirn Lodge and Midmar Forest and his uncle's life and his aunty's suppers. But what pleased him most of all was the thought of once again seeing the light in his mother's eyes, and her leaving the backroom, the refuge. And his father taking him fishing and to football matches.

"I'll go to school tomorrow, Mum. Promise."

There were only a few days of term left before the Christmas holidays. It was something.

The shadow of the bird didn't return that day.

Miss Lewis stood behind her desk, arms folded, as the children filed in. In her classroom everything was orderly. She stood no nonsense. Her expression, rather stern, remained fixed – until Archie Edgar appeared. He tried to blend in with the rest, but it didn't work.

He stood out. He glared. His flame-red hair always was a giveaway. Couldn't be anyone but Archie.

Miss Lewis's eyebrows seemed to lift half an inch. The missing person was back. The wanderer had returned. The class, for once, was complete.

"Archie! Lovely to see you!"

He kept his head down and went to the desk that so rarely saw any books or pencils sprawled across it. He couldn't tell whether the teacher was pleased to see him or merely poking fun. It didn't matter; he was there. He promised his mother he would go. And Rosie.

One boy leaned across the aisle and whispered, "Why yer come now, Edgar, only two days to end of term?" His voice was like barbed wire.

On his other side was Agnie Robson. Although Archie stared down at the unscuffed varnish on his desk, he felt Agnie's eyes upon him like blazing headlights.

The day started with 'News Time'. It got everyone warmed up in a gentle way. In strict rotation, pupils were asked to tell of something that had pleased them, or seemed terribly important, during the previous week. Some stories were sad and serious, some provoked huge outbursts of laughter, and some were obviously exaggerated.

Miss Lewis said, "Archie, as we haven't had the pleasure of your company for some time, perhaps you could think of something recent in your life that you could tell as all about."

Archie lifted his head and looked about the class. Every pupil was silent, staring at him. "Me, Miss?"

"Why not, Archie?"

He thought of Rosie, the vanished one and the promised one.

No, he couldn't.

Then he thought of Uncle Craig and the owl's nest. The silence stretched out painfully.

"Well, Archie?"

He heard boys mumbling. "Go on, Edgar, tell us a joke." And worse suggestions. He felt as if he'd stepped into a furnace. Or a bear-pit.

Then he said, "There is something, Miss."

"Go on, Archie, we're all waiting."

"It was last Saturday, Miss."

Another silence. Boys mumbling. Girls tutting with impatience. Agnie Robson staring a hole right through him.

"We're listening hard to every word, Archie."

He concentrated on the wooden surface of the desk. It was mottled like plumage. "I was at my Uncle Craig's cottage in Midmar Forest. . . I always stay there on Friday nights. . . My Aunty Brenda makes fish supper. . ."

A boy behind him whispered. "Get on wi' it. Edgar, or we'll miss playtime."

"As I said, Miss, I was with my Uncle Craig. . . Out early. Snow on the ground. . . He took me right into the forest, further than I'd ever been, and. . . and we stopped at the base of a big tree and Uncle Craig said look down there, Archie, what do you see? And I stared at the patch of ground sprinkled with snow and. . ."

A boy across the class shouted, "And it was a giant grizzly bear. Grrr!"

The whole class erupted in laughter.

Miss Lewis raised her voice above the din. "Mackie, keep your tongue to yourself!" Laughter turned instantly to silence. "Archie, continue."

"Well, Miss, I stared and stared and couldn't make out much until my Uncle Craig made me look harder. Then I made out an old nest, all untidy and scattered about. And there were little bones around it. . ."

Another boy whispered aloud in a creepy voice. "A human skeleton!"

More general laughter.

Miss Lewis glared at the boy. It was enough. The boy's head seemed to shrink down into his neck.

"Uncle Craig told me it was the old nest of a long-eared owl. Sometimes they make them on the ground in other birds' nests. It had five eggs in it last spring, Miss, and ma uncle watched them hatch and develop into owlets. . ."

Miss Lewis said, "Go on, Archie."

Archie looked up from the surface of the desk and said, "That's it, Miss."

"That supposed to be news, Edgar?" It was Mackie again. Mackie couldn't keep quiet for long. "Soppy birds' nests! That's no news, Miss, that isn't! We want to hear about a trip to Ibrox!"

All the boys and girls began rumbling and making hooting noises – all except Agnie Robson, who announced loudly in a grown-up voice, "I think that's a lovely story, Miss Lewis." Agnie's voice made Archie cringe; it was so sweet and loving. And yet he had to be grateful for her support.

Miss Lewis clapped her hands once and glared and turned mutiny into total silence.

"Welcome back to the class, Archie Edgar. It took some courage to tell us your news."

Archie's uncertain smile was a rare event.

It felt like some kind of victory.

Dear Rory,

I can't write much this time. Its friday again and Ace is picking me up soon. I went to skool yesterday. I tried to slip into my place but Harpy knew straigth away. Didnt you ever go to skool befor your imprisonment.

Harpy picked on me staigth away. Newstime. First thing. Always is. I told them all about the owls nest and they larfed. why The only one to say something nice was Pain, of all peeple. It made my feelings all mix up.

I only went as a promise to Number One. I wish I didnt see so many bottels in her room. And the pong of all that strong stuff. But she promised to bring Rosie back which is like promising a miracel. And they dont happen do they. You mite know that Rory stuck in your place. One day the tree will let you go. Ill help if I can.

I can hear Aces Landrover pulling up out the front. Cant wait. Keep watch over me, Rory

Your frend Archie

CHAPTER SIX

'Free'

As usual Archie's heartbeat rattled like a coin in an empty tin.

The Land Rover engine died. There it was: a knock on the door. More or less the same time every Friday. Uncle Craig came in and spoke to Dodie Edgar. Archie overheard from the top of the stairs.

"How's Mollie, then?"

"Oh, she's in the backroom."

It was a strange reply, not really an answer. Or rather, it sent the message: nothing's changed.

"And how're you, Dodie?"

"Bearing up, Craig. You know."

"Got another job yet?"

"Nay job. Nothing around Aberdeen since they shut down the rigs, is there?"

"So it's tea and telly," Uncle Craig joked.

"Aye." Dodie Edgar seemed a little ashamed to admit it, especially to his brother-in-law who spent such an active life. He and Aunty Brenda hardly ever watched television. In the Midmar Forest there were better things to do and they were so busy anyway.

Archie loved the peace and quiet there, inside the lodge and out: just the soft babble of real conversation and forest sounds, not the artificial squeak and boom and jangle of the television set sitting in a corner of the room like a big blue eye having a fit.

Just before Uncle Craig left with Archie and his rucksack, he popped his head in the living room door. Dodie Edgar was already pointing the remote. Lights skipped all around the walls. Some crazy gameshow was on.

"Say hello to Mollie for me. I'll bring Little'un back on the dot tomorrow afternoon. By the way, thinking of jobs – I might have something for you. Give me a bit o' time to sort it out. See you, Dodie."

But Dodie Edgar was mesmerised by the images on the screen. He didn't take long to cast a spell on himself.

Archie shouted from the hall, "Bye, Dad! See you tomorrow!" He didn't go into the sitting room. There was no point. His father wouldn't hug him or give him a peck on the cheek. Nothing like that. At ten he was too old for soppiness.

After Aunty Brenda's fish supper, Uncle Craig took Archie out through the back of the lodge. He'd told his nephew to wrap up warm or else he'd catch a death. Archie was puzzled. That late on a Friday evening they didn't go out. It was dark and confusing amongst the surrounding conifers. They always waited until bright and early Saturday morning, when Uncle Craig could point things out. When Archie could look up and see the sky high above the wavering trees, for it was nearly always windy with a breeze reaching ten miles off the North Sea. Pushing inland, the smell of salt still in it.

Uncle Craig wielded the torch and Archie followed.

There was something magical about the forest after dark. Especially when snow lay on the ground. Everything looked so different. It became another world, with altered shapes and colours. It was dreamlike.

Archie saw the wooden door in a pool of light.

He knew where the old shed was but had never paid it much attention. Full of rusty tools, he imagined, and cobwebs.

Uncle Craig raised a hand to the shed door. He lightly tapped his fingers on it, which seemed odd to Archie. It was like a password.

"Prepare for a surprise."

Archie began to feel worried. The coin in the empty tin rattled again. He stood behind his uncle for safety and leaned to one side and peered at the slats of the door in the juddery pool of light.

The door seemed to creak open of its own accord. Magic again. A conjuring trick.

Two reflective unblinking saucers stared right into him. Night-eyes. Startling. Yellow and piercing. Archie felt chilled, rooted, enchanted. Eyes that hovered in the dark. But he knew immediately.

In a voice full of wonder, Archie whispered, "Uncle Craig!"

"Yes, Little'un – a long-eared owl. Trained as a man can make it."

"Those eyes! Staring. Beautiful. Like two moons."

"They see everything. But I'm probably blinding her with this torch. She doesn't seem too disturbed, does she? I was a bit afraid. How she'd react and that."

Uncle Craig played torchlight around the owl's body.

"She's yours, Little'un, at least for a while."

Archie's voice was full of wonder. "Mine?"

"I've trained her up. Secretly. Eight months of sweat. Now you take over."

"But. . ."

"Don't worry, I'll show you everything."

The pair of golden eyes stared back at Archie. It felt as if the world had changed. In one moment everything had shifted a gear. From loss to love.

Saturday morning the skies were clear blue above Midmar Forest. Conifers sang in the breeze, swayed in a slow-motion dance.

Archie breathed deeply, seemed to suck in the whole forest air. This was better than the city, than the sea even. And with the owl it was better still. Life, recently so topsy-turvy, turned right way up.

Uncle Craig brought her slowly out of the shed, as though she were fragile porcelain that might break. When the owl exercised her wings it startled Archie. He felt a powerful draught. He studied the bird in dappled sunlight and found himself speechless. She seemed more wonderful than anything he'd ever seen.

Then he thought of Rosie. And under the joy a sliver of sadness slipped.

"There we are, Little'un. Early Christmas present."

"Uncle Craig, she's. . ." Archie racked his brains for a suitable word.

"Don't even try to say it. Just watch and wonder, as I do."

"Can I name her? Can I?"

Uncle Craig laughed. "Well, she hasn't got one at the moment."

"I don't know what to call her."

"No rush."

The bird sat impassively on Uncle Craig's forearm, which the leather gauntlet gripped. When it swivelled its head, Archie's eyes nearly popped out.

"How did it do that?"

"No problem for an owl. Like a radar scanner, goes round and round. Neck like a corkscrew! Needs to see everything, like. Mice, rats, birds – even humans."

Archie was horrified. "To eat?"

Uncle Craig stifled a chuckle. "Rats and mice – yes. Humans – what do you think?"

Archie studied the owl's plumage. She was superb. A feathery sculpture. She was slender rather than round. Her plumage was mottled, almost like the tortoiseshell cat along the street. With burning amber eyes she looked fierce, alarmed, and yet he knew she was relaxed. And those ear tufts! That's what singled her out, gave her final beauty. Standing erect like tapered lengths of brown cotton wool. That's what gave her her name. They were pretend ears, but no less amazing for that.

Archie wanted to stroke her head but was a little afraid.

Reading his mind, Uncle Craig said, "Go on, then."

"What?"

"Stroke her, Little'un. She's got used to you already."

Archie took one step forward. He lifted his hand high over her head with great delicacy. She didn't move; she simply stared. He lowered his fingers and tickled between the tufts. The feeling was incredible: soft like those fluffy blankets babies are wrapped in. Like silk.

Uncle Craig took Archie to the Meadow, the broad clearing walled with conifers. He gave instructions.

"Stand at the edge and just watch closely."

Uncle Craig stood dead centre of the clearing. He stretched out the arm on which the owl sat. Archie held in his excitement. The owl's head swivelled once in a nearly complete circle and back again. Sunshine struck her plumage and the mottled brown seemed to glow like gold.

Uncle Craig clucked his teeth a few times and raised the arm which had become a perch. Archie stared as the owl's wings outstretched and flapped and her talons loosened from the gauntlet and she rose a foot above Uncle Craig and then dived sideways. And before Archie realised it, the owl was careering around on a straight leash, describing one circle after another. The great wings flapping, the bird's body dipping to skim the earth, the draught like a warm wind as she passed within arm's length of Archie.

When Uncle Craig had finished the demonstration he gradually shortened the leash and eased the bird towards him. The flight circle got smaller and smaller, until the owl fluttered in a mass of down onto his forearm and Uncle Craig ducked his head to one side to avoid the beating wings.

Archie walked to the middle of the Meadow.

Uncle Craig smiled as the owl settled.

"There, Little'un. What do you think?"

Archie was breathless. "Can I do that, Uncle Craig?"

"Sure, sure. Give it time. No rush."

The owl now sat as still and calm as before. Archie gently lifted his hand and touched the bird's glittering breast plumage. Yes, just like silk. She seemed to stare right through him.

"I know what to call her, Uncle Craig."

"Go on, surprise me."

"I'll call her. . . Free."

Uncle Craig laughed. Gently teasing, he said, "Free? And I've got her imprisoned on a leash?"

"I know she's not free now – but one day she will be."

CHAPTER SEVEN

'What?'

Uncle Craig dropped Archie back home after lunch-time on Saturday. The boy's head swam full of owl images. His heart was full of everything. He was overflowing in a way it was impossible to put into words. And yet he had to return to the city, his home, the bustle and clank and smoke of buildings and yards and the looming sea.

He stood at the front door and waved at the rear window of Uncle Craig's Land Rover. Then he went into the sitting-room.

"Archie, ma boy, you're back! The wanderer returns!"

Dodie Edgar lay sprawled across the settee, legs dangling off the end. An empty crisp packet lay on the carpet next to a half drunk glass of beer.

"Hi, Dad!"

Dodie Edgar swung his legs off the settee and patted the newly vacant cushion. "Come and park yoursel' next to your old Daddy, Arch."

With the curtains only slightly parted, the sitting-room was semi-dark, lit by the glare of the television.

Archie went reluctantly to sit next to his father.

"Have a good time at your uncle and aunty's?"

Archie was dying to mention the long-eared owl. He was brimming with the sheer thrill of that memory of first seeing her, and then watching her circle like a blaze of golden brown in the Meadow.

But he knew his father wouldn't listen. Or he would just say 'Great!' without thinking, as if that was a real reply. All Archie did was stare at the flickering screen, looking without seeing. It numbed him.

"Come on then, boy, hutch up against me. Footba' Review'll be on soon. You love footba', don't you?"

"Aye, Dad."

Archie felt empty, almost like part of the furniture. He remembered the days when his father went out to work early in the morning on the oil rig, and how sometimes he had to stay at sea all week, and Archie would catch up with him on Saturday afternoons when his father took him to a match and joked with him and made him laugh from beginning to end. And then on Saturdays they went fishing if the weather wasn't horribly cold or wet, and sometimes they went even then. He thought of those as the 'old days', although it was barely a year ago, before Rosie came and went.

The familiar theme music for Football Review flooded the sitting-room. The volume was ear-splitting. Archie felt the whole house shake. His head was so full of the noise that it crowded out images of the owl. It was too harsh, too much in-your –face. It didn't seem real.

At the end of Football Review, Dodie Edgar did something that took Archie totally by surprise: he switched off the television.

An eerie silence descended on the sitting-room. Archie stared at the walls, the curtains, each object in turn. He could barely see them now that the glare had gone. But everything looked different, softer, calmer, more settled. As if the sitting-room had been returned to itself again, given back its soul.

He connected that to the time when his mother used to sit in there with him, and they would chatter quietly about anything that came into their heads. And slanted shafts of sunshine came through the window and made bright pools on the carpet.

Dodie Edgar turned to his son.

"Now then, Archie. It's nearly Christmas. You know I haven't been working for a while, but I've got some redundancy money; we're not dirt poor yet. What do you want?"

Archie thought, Want? He echoed his father's words. All he wanted was Free, the long-eared owl, and a cottage in Midmar Forest, and an uncle who might become, through some sort of miracle, his father. Practically, though, he wanted his own gauntlet and leash and a really up to date book on owls and maybe some coloured pencils and a special pad to draw pictures of them and make notes.

"Dad, I think I'd like. . ."

His father raised a hand like a traffic policeman. "Halt! Say no more! I've already thought about it."

"You have?"

"Yes. – A computer. I've got the money. Stick it in your bedroom, Arch, and it'll teach you all that stuff you're missing at school. Help you catch up."

"But, Dad. . ."

"I've been reading it up. You don't really need school these days. It's all there at your fingertips. Information. Anything you want to know. Anything in the world. I read, 'You can bring the whole world into your own home'." Dodie Edgar smiled in triumph. "How about that? Magic, eh?"

Archie didn't know what to say. He felt he ought to be grateful. But he didn't feel grateful. He felt confused, almost cheated. He'd been asked what he wanted – and then told.

When Dodie Edgar saw the open-mouthed expression on his son's face, he said, "Well, think about it. We've got a week, haven't we?"

Archie heard the knock on the front door from his bedroom. He'd been lying on his bed with his hands behind his head and his eyes closed, imagining Free in flight. He'd been thinking of going to the backroom and telling his mother what Uncle Craig had given him. But he didn't want to see the darkness behind her eyes. He didn't want to catch a whiff of wine or gin or whatever it was this week. He knew that only half of her would be there; the other half was always somewhere else.

It was Agnie Robson again.

She always called at Archie's house. Every week. She was more regular than the postman and the milkman lumped together. But she didn't deliver anything but a sickly smile and a sort of twisted friendship.

"Hello, Archie." She stood a pace away from the doorstep.

"I can't come to school today, Ag."

Agnie said sweetly, "Nor can I."

"What?" Archie felt confused. (Why was life so confusing?)

"School finished last Friday, the day after you told us all about the owl's nest. It's Christmas holidays now."

"Oh." Inwardly Archie began to panic. (More confusion.) "Well, Ag, what do you want?"

"I want to hear more about owls."

"What?"

"Owls."

"I heard you."

"Why did you say 'what', then?"

"I don't know."

Agnie noticed Archie's face gradually turning as red as his hair. Soon he'll look like a tomato, she thought. His freckles were vanishing. The blue of his eyes stood out more. His mouth was opening and closing like a goldfish's, but no words were coming out.

"Is there something wrong with you, Archie? Are you ill?"

"No, Ag, I just don't feel like coming out – or talking about owls."

"You never do."

"What?"

Agnie stuck her hands on her hips and looked up to heaven in exasperation. It was a perfect impersonation of Miss Lewis. "There you go again!"

Archie didn't understand. "What?"

"Every other word is a 'What', Archie Edgar. You're impossible!" She sounded so old-fashioned. Agnie reminded Archie of a little old lady. She'd be perfect in the school play as one of the ugly sisters.

But then, as usual, Archie felt guilty.

"Ag. . ."

"What?"

He smiled. "Now *you're* saying it!"

She smiled too, covering her mouth with one hand. "Oops!"

"Thanks for sticking up for me in class." He had to push himself hard to come out with that. He had to swallow a lot of pride. It was never easy, especially with Agnie Robson.

33

Like a grown-up, with her nose in the air, she said, "Don't mention it."

The two children looked at each other. Chatter had died a death. There seemed nothing more to say. The colour in Archie's face had returned to normal. His freckles reflected daylight. His hair spiked and glistened.

"Not coming out, then?"

"No, Ag, ma Dad's taking me footy and ma Mum's. . ."

Agnie knew all about Mrs Edgar. Everybody did. You didn't say anything about Mrs Edgar. Not these days.

"Okay." Agnie tried to sound cheerful, as if it didn't matter. "I'll come around again in the holidays, eh? Happy Christmas, Arch!"

Archie simply stared after Agnie as she walked along the pavement. When she turned round he ducked his head in the door. He swore he wouldn't tell anyone about owls again.

Except his mother.

CHAPTER EIGHT

Two Items of News

Archie couldn't wait until Friday. But he had to.

He hoped that Christmas wouldn't change the weekend routine. The trouble was, it always did. At Christmas everything went topsy-turvy again. Strangers came and went, people you vaguely remembered from a year ago, or from weddings and funerals. People who smiled and pinched your cheek and pressed a few coins in your hand and said your name, and you didn't have a clue what theirs was. People who were part of a family you hardly ever saw and yet behaved as if you came across them every day.

So Christmas was a kind of mixed joy and worry for Archie.

He sat at the bottom of the stairs, his elbows on his knees, his chin cupped in his hands, as if his head was too heavy for his neck to support. Thinking. Thinking when he really wanted to be doing.

Then, out of the corner of an eye, he caught sight of his mother gliding along the hall from the backroom to the kitchen. She seemed to move soundlessly like a ghost, lighter than air. She never seemed to stumble.

Archie followed her into the kitchen. She stood with her back to him, fiddling at the sink. He watched her for a long time. He just wanted to study his mother without disturbing her. If he did that she might glide right back to her room.

She seemed stick-thin these days. Her hair was as throwaway at the back as it was at the front. She seemed to lean to one side as if squeezing a pain. Her movements were quick, sharp, agitated. Like a bird's. And yet not graceful. She fiddled with something hidden. He could hear her voice. She seemed to be cursing to herself.

Archie couldn't bear it any longer. The one word came out. "Mum?"

She spun around with amazing speed. Faced him, startled, her eyes blazing. In her hands she held an unopened bottle. Archie stared at it. It contained a colourless liquid. He didn't know what it was, but it was nothing like lemonade. He imagined it burning her insides.

"Archie, don't creep up on me like that!"

"Mum, I didn't mean to. . ."

"You could've given me a heart attack!"

"What?" He didn't understand. That word again. The old confusion. The fear.

"Never mind." Mrs Edgar put the bottle on the draining-board. "Look, Archie, come into my room. I need to speak to you."

"About what?"

"I need to tell you something. Really important."

They walked down the hall. The sound of a TV comedy came muffled from the sitting-room. Dodie Edgar's laughter punched holes in the soundtrack. The house was filled with strangeness.

Mollie Edgar sat her son down in her bedside chair. It was old and he felt the springs pinch his bottom. She knelt on the floor, her knees touching the toes of his socks. She'd never done that before. She made it so that her face was lower than his. As if she were praying. She cleared her throat.

"Archie, you're going to have another sister."

"What?"

"Didn't you hear me? Sister."

It couldn't be. Things didn't happen like that. They took time.

"You mean Rosie's coming back?"

"Not exactly."

"You mean someone just like her?"

"I hope so."

"When?"

"Soon."

"For Christmas?"

"Not that soon."

"When?"

"Let's see. About May."

"When's that?"

"About five months' time."

Archie thought his mother was too thin. He remembered how much she grew, in every direction except up, before Rosie came. How her walk changed. How she leaned backwards to stretch and her back hurt a lot and her clothes wouldn't fit. How she was so careful about what she ate and drank.

She took his hands in hers. He looked into her eyes and thought he saw a glint instead of the dullness and the haze. (A bird fluttered back into her.)

"Can we call her Rosie, too?"

Mollie Edgar smiled. "We haven't decided. We'll see."

When Archie saw his mother smile, *he* smiled. She looked more human when she smiled. She looked as though she could take flight.

"How about Dad?"

Archie wondered how the howling of a baby might affect his television watching.

"He says I must get rid of the bottles straight away."

The coin rattled in the empty tin of Archie's heart. "Will you, Mum? Will you?"

She said, "Do you know why I stood at the sink?"

"To open a bottle. But you couldn't."

"No. And what would I have done if I'd unscrewed the top?"

"Drunk. . ."

"No! Poured it all down the sink. I swear."

Archie shuffled on the springs and looked down and studied her face and really didn't know whether to believe her. He wanted to.

All this felt painful, so he said, "I've got something important to tell *you*, Mum."

"You have?" Archie nodded. "Go on, then."

"An early Christmas present from Uncle Craig."

"Don't tell me. A tree-feller's axe."

"No."

"Your own Land Rover."

Archie burst into laughter. "No!"

"I give up."

"Already?"

"Yes."

"A long-eared owl."

"What?" That favourite word sounded peculiar in his mother's tone of voice.

"A long-eared owl."

"I didn't know owls had long ears."

"They don't. They call them ears but really they're little pointy feathers on the top of their heads."

Mollie Edgar looked suspiciously at her son, not quite believing.

"How do you know all this?"

"Library books and Uncle Craig."

Mollie Edgar began to push herself up from the carpet. She gripped her stomach and winced. Even though she was thin there was a kind of heaviness in her. Archie could see it and he could feel it when he took one of her arms and said, "Let me help you, Mum."

"Thanks, Arch."

When she was finally upright she towered over him.

Archie wasn't quite sure how she took the owl business. And Mollie Edgar wasn't sure what Archie thought of another Rosie. Two items of news. Two things to sink in. Two changes.

Mollie Edgar stared down at her son. Her serious expression made him feel that she must be angry until she broke into a broad, sunny smile, the best he'd seen in weeks, months, a whole year.

"Archie Edgar, you're an amazing little tyke!"

When he left the back room he didn't quite know what to do, where to go. The sudden surge of happiness stopped him doing anything in particular. He just wanted to bathe in it.

Eventually, his mind settling, his heart steadying, he went to his bedroom and got out the notepad with the elasticated clasp and the tucked-in pencil. He sprawled on his bed. Tapping the lead of his pencil on his lower lip, he tried to think of the correct order of events to tell his imprisoned friend.

Dear Rory,

Things keep happening. I can't keep up. I wish I could visit you, or you visit me. Everything's upside down again. The whole world. Where does it begin and where does it end? I keep thinking this. Am I silly? Am I mad? Every day my heart does a different dance.

Uncle Craig drove me to his house in the forest last week. I thought it was going to be normal (that's exciting enough). But Uncle Craig took me outside when it was dark and cold. I got worried. We went to his garden shed. He opened the door and shone the torch in and I got the shock of my life. An owl was staring at us. It sat on a perch and its eyes were made of gold and hovered in the dark like two planets in space.

Next morning (Saturday) we went out to the shed. By now it was daylight. Uncle Craig brought the owl outside. He'd trained it. It sat on his arm on a huge glove. He told me she (it was a femal long eared owl) was my speshal Christmas present. I kept looking and couldent say a word, not even thank you. Uncle Craig had trianed her in secret for months. He's like a crafty majishun.

Then we went to the meadow (a big forest cleering) and he put on a show. The owl flew on a circel on a long lead at such supersonic speed it was a blurr. I was dieing to fly her myself. But I needed training and pashence.

I named my long eared owl Free. I now that sounds silly becos she's not free. She will be one day thogh. We will all be wont we? Even you Rory.

Dad wants to by me a compooter for Christmas. I'd rather have all those things that go with owls – I mean real things that you can do outside. I prefer being outside. Sitting still is a nusance and makes you yawn.

Agnie Robson came knocking on our front door again. She made me feel bad. I cant stand her really but she was the only one in class who didn't larf when I talked about owls in newstime. I still cant stand her.

But at least I can see now that she means well.

I'm saving the best till last (I think its the best). Mum said were going to get Rosie back – well not exactly. She meant a brand new

Rosie. Next year. I saw a kind of light in her eyes so it must be true. If I get a sketchpad Ill draw Free and Rosie 2.

Rory it must be aweful being stuck in one position. If someone cuts the tree down, slip out wont you?

Your frend Archie

CHAPTER NINE

An Unexpected Gift

Archie could hardly hear his father's voice over the din of the television. Why didn't he ever turn it off?

"A quiet Christmas this year. Aren't you listening?"

Archie had been trying to listen, but the images on the screen drew his eyes with magnetic force, and he couldn't help listening to the voices in dramatic conversation. That's what it did to you – blotted everything else out.

Dodie Edgar raised his voice. "I said aren't you listening?"

"Yes, Dad."

"Well, you're not saying anything."

Archie had fallen into a trance. "About what, Dad?"

Steam came out of Dodie Edgar's ears. "About Christmas!" he yelled.

Gormlessly, Archie said, "It's only in a few days, isn't it?"

Dodie Edgar was getting nowhere with his son.

The sitting-room glowed and buzzed. Archie couldn't stand it anymore so he rushed out the door and dashed straight up the stairs and ran into his bedroom and fell right across the bed and burst into tears. He hadn't done that for ages. He had bottled every feeling up, swallowed hard and tried to be brave every time a hint of tears came near him. But now he felt like a dam which had burst and gushed its waters everywhere.

The voice at the door didn't help. It was hard rather than forgiving. "Why are you crying like a wee baby, Archie Edgar?" his father asked.

Archie flipped over on the bed and yelled, "Because you don't understand!"

Dodie Edgar's mouth fell open and his eyes widened. He'd never been spoken to like that. Suddenly he realised. He stopped himself shouting in return. In the sitting-room it wouldn't be like this, just the two of them, just the quiet.

He went without a sound over to the bed and sat next to his son and tried to give him a hug. Archie resisted, but then allowed his father to take his head softly in his hands, just as his mother had done. It was a homecoming.

Dodie Edgar explained in a hushed voice, "We have to have a quiet Christmas because of your mother, son."

Archie wiped an arm across his face. Tears blurred his eyes. He looked up at his father and said, "I know about the next Rosie, Dad."

Now his father knew what had burst the dam.

"It's true, Arch – another wee sister. In May."

"But Mum won't. . ."

"Yes she will. She'll no drink anymore. Not now she knows. She's something to look forward to. And the backroom'll be a nursery again, same as it was a year ago."

Archie still felt desperate. "But, Dad, you haven't got a. . ."

"Job?" He laughed. "Oh, don't fret so. I will have. Your Uncle Craig's going to see about it. Nowhere near the oil rigs this time. On dry land."

Archie tried to smile. His watery vision distorted everything. Uncle Craig to the rescue. He *was* a 'wise man', a kind of super owl, swivelling his head and seeing everything and fixing life for people. Magic. Miracles.

"Uncle Craig can do anything, Dad."

Dodie Edgar smiled as he ruffled Archie's hair. "Well, *nearly* everything.

Archie heard a knock at the front door. On Christmas Eve it wouldn't be carol singers, too late for that. Then he thought: Uncle Craig and Aunty Brenda have come early. They're going to stay overnight!

He knew his mother wouldn't leave the backroom to answer the door. She never did. And his father couldn't hear outside sounds above the noise of the television. It always seemed to be up to Archie.

When he swung the front door open he was beaming. He had adjusted his eyes to look at the height where adult faces would appear, but there was only dark sky. Then his eyes dropped to the shadowy face of Agnie Robson.

"Hello, Archie."

He was amazed and confused. "You! It's Christmas Eve, Ag, what do *you* want?"

"That's nice Archie Edgar," she said. "Can't you say 'Merry Christmas' or something?"

"No!"

"That's nice, I must say!"

"Don't keep saying 'that's nice'. What do you want, Ag?"

She looked past him, down the hall. Nosey. "Are you busy?"

"Yes." He wasn't, hadn't a thing to do. But he wanted to get rid of her. You don't have school friends, or enemies, calling round on Christmas Eve for no reason. "I'm wrapping presents."

Agnie said, "I was just passing."

"Well, you can pass without knocking on the door."

However cruel Archie was to Agnie, she didn't seem to notice. Or she chose to ignore him. 'Thick-skinned' his father called such people.

"Don't be mad, Arch."

"I'm not mad, I'm busy."

She ignored him. "I stuck up for you that one day you came to school, when you talked about owls in News Time."

"So." She was making him feel bad. She was clever at doing that.

"So I wanted to know if you could tell me anymore."

It was freezing cold at the front door. A mighty draught was sweeping down the hall. It would have been nice near the fire.

"Not now, Ag, it's Christmas Eve."

"Doesn't matter when it is."

"Course it does."

All this time Agnie had had her hands behind her back. Archie hadn't noticed.

Suddenly she brought both hands out of hiding. Archie found a neatly gift-wrapped little parcel shining in the dark in front of his eyes. It had a silver bow on the top. He didn't know what to say or do.

Agnie tried a smile. "Happy Christmas, Archie!"

He felt terrible: confused, guilty, all kinds of things he couldn't explain wrapped into one. What was she trying to do?

She shoved the present into his hands and turned away quite suddenly as if there was something wrong. Archie stood there like a dumb fool, the gift reflecting street lights and Agnie already half way down the pavement.

He went up to his bedroom and ripped off the gift wrap. He found himself staring at a beautiful snow-white image of a bird with amber eyes. He read the book's title: 'Owls: a Handbook'.

CHAPTER TEN

Something That Captures Your Mind

Uncle Craig and Aunty Brenda arrived early on Christmas morning. They were early for everything. They couldn't have been more different than Archie's parents.

Something always felt wrong when Archie was with his aunt and uncle and his parents all together. He felt torn. He felt like two different people in the same body. It didn't happen very often, these days only once a year. At least the television might die a death. At least his mother would emerge from the backroom and stay put, maybe for hours.

Archie lay flat on his bed, dressed but still sleepy. He couldn't get over the owl book. He couldn't get over Agnie's visit. Whenever he pushed an ear into the mattress, it acted like a big sound box, similar to pressing your ear against a wall. He could hear all the downstairs voices, muffled but understandable. It was a game he loved, like spying, eavesdropping. He felt like a nesting creature.

They all sat around the dining-table in the sitting room. Dodie Edgar had put the flaps up and dusted it down and stuck the only clean table cloth he could find on it. It didn't quite cover the table. He had to do things that Mollie Edgar used to do, before Rosie was taken away.

Five of them around the table.

Archie's face hardly rose above the surface. Three of the adults seemed enormous, loud, overpowering. His mother hardly said a word. He couldn't make out much of what they were talking about. Only snatches.

Nothing seemed jolly or joyful. He yearned for someone his own age, or even close to it. The chatter went over his head. He even cast his mind back to Agnie Robson, and wished now that she were sitting next to him and that he was telling her about Free and the clearing in Midmar Forest and the blur of living light which formed a circle on the tightened leash. But she wasn't there. She'd scooted away from the front door quickly and all he had was the Owl Handbook, which was lovely but burned his fingers with guilt whenever he touched it.

Archie remembered stuffing himself with Christmas dinner and murmuring Yes or No whenever someone asked him a question. He felt tied to the leg of the table. In the sitting room he felt like a caged bird. Everything and everyone seemed pulled tight, on a leash of their own, as far as you could get from free. On their best behaviour, like circus animals.

He left the dining table as soon as his father gave him the nod. It was the first time he'd ever forgotten that Uncle Craig was around. His uncle seemed for once an ordinary man, a member of the family, not a magician who could put everything right with a click of his fingers.

When Archie got to his bedroom he found the computer already set up on his chest of drawers in a corner of the room. His father had shifted the pebbles and feathers and bits of driftwood that Archie always arranged neatly there. Shoved them into the top drawer. As if they meant nothing. He was always reminding Archie to 'get rid of all that rubbish, you'd bring the mud in if you could'.

He looked at the blank screen. It showed a reflection of himself. The light streaming in the window was strong. All those dangling wires made him feel uneasy. What were they all for? It felt like a stranger in his room.

Because he rarely attended school, Archie was unfamiliar with computers. He hadn't wanted one for Christmas. He hadn't liked the thought of sitting in one place staring into an illuminated square. It was a pretend world. It reminded him too much of the television, of his father's glue-eyes. Like something that captures your mind, that you can't escape from. He was so relieved when he heard Uncle Craig calling him.

When Archie reached the bottom of the stairs, Uncle Craig was smiling as if he'd won the Lottery. He patted his stomach.

"All that food, Little'un. Making them doze off in there, even your Aunty Brenda. I need to walk if off. Fancy a trot down to the sea?"

Archie didn't need asking twice.

They reached the harbour through side streets. There wasn't a soul in sight. Archie had never seen the place so deserted. It was strange yet exciting. Everyone must be sleeping off their Christmas dinners, or goggling at the Queen delivering her message, or tearing the paper off presents saved for later. It left the city and the seafront to gulls. And to them.

Uncle Craig took Archie over to a wooden bench. They sat in the bitter cold. Uncle Craig put an arm around Archie's shoulders and hugged him because he knew how chilly it felt now that they were still.

"Well, then, Little'un. Things aren't too good, are they?"

"What?" Archie didn't quite grasp the question.

"You're all mixed up, aren't you?"

"What do you mean, Uncle Craig?"

"I know all about it. Life's topsy-turvy at the moment. I can figure out more than you think."

Was he a mind-reader as well?

Archie stared at the sea.

He felt something like a wave rising through his body.

Uncle Craig looked down at him.

"It'll be all right, Little'un. In the end. Everything is. I take a wee peek at the Good Book every now and then."

"The what?"

"The Bible."

"Oh. That."

"Yes. That."

"What does it say, Uncle Craig?"

"It says all things must pass. And it says a lot more." He waved an arm right across the sea. "All this is temporary."

Temporary? It made Archie feel worse. He didn't want the good things to vanish. Good things were forever. Like his uncle. Like the long-eared owl. Like the Rosie yet to come.

"But Uncle..."

"Don't fret. It all makes sense. If you see everything in the right way, it all fits together properly. Like a complicated puzzle. For most people there are ever so many parts missing. They can never manage to see the whole thing. One day, if you're lucky, you pop the final piece into the puzzle and you stand back and you suddenly see the complete picture. Nothing missing. Magic!"

Although Archie didn't understand much of this, he was impressed.

The wave that had come up to his throat and tightened it into a point of pain sank down again. He knew he'd come close to tears. On Christmas Day, too. He almost felt ashamed of himself.

Gulls wheeled and shrieked close around the bench. Hungry. Dive bombing. Archie studied them, and then he said, "Uncle Craig, when am I going to see Free again?"

"Tomorrow. I knew you'd ask. Not a Friday but it's been agreed. Weren't you listening at the dinner table?"

Archie thought: tomorrow. Boxing Day. Out in the forest. Flying the owl. That will be the perfect present. And then his mind slipped into thinking about his mother and the future Rosie and the wave crept up through his body again and some force almost grabbed him by the throat.

He walked back through side streets to the house with Uncle Craig's arm still across his shoulders. The sea wind had been left behind.

When they got in the house all was still and quiet. Not even the television was on.

CHAPTER ELEVEN

Electric Power

Back in the Midmar Forest. At last! Archie felt that Christmas Day just hadn't worked. Nothing in the jigsaw quite fitted. Some of the best pieces were upside down. Or just missing.

He felt guilty, though: Boxing Day and he wasn't at home. His mother had retired to the backroom straight after lunch, groaning and rubbing her stomach and saying it was all too much. He saw her take a bottle with her.

His father got up and burped and switched on the television as soon as the trifle had been guzzled and said, "Let's see what golden oldies are on. They usually put some classics on at Christmas."

That's when Archie had noticed Uncle Craig catch Aunty Brenda's eye and raise his own eyes to the ceiling as if to say, 'Oh no, not the dreaded box!' That's when he'd taken Archie for a walk down to the harbour and the gulls had cried and the freedom of the sea seemed even bigger than the freedom of the forest.

Uncle Craig took Archie back to the garden shed. He tapped lightly on the door three times. The password. The little noise that meant, 'It's okay, a friend is here'.

Archie whispered, "Can we take her to the Meadow, Uncle Craig?"

He whispered back as he gently opened the shed door, "You read my mind, Little'un."

"And can *I* fly her this time?"

"Be prepared. This is what we've come for. Your turn." And then, pretend serious, "Are you man enough?"

Archie felt a great surge of breath drawn into his body. He felt dizzy. His excitement nearly exploded out of him, but he knew he needed to keep control for Free's sake. You had to tread carefully with wild creatures.

The shed door was wide open.

Uncle Craig stepped in.

Everything lay in deep shadow.

When Archie tried to squeeze in, Uncle Craig said, "Wait! Two of us in this small space'll spook her. I'll bring her out into daylight."

Archie waited.

The cold canopy of the forest held its breath.

Archie heard a metallic click as Uncle Craig attached the leash to the owl's swivel, which was fixed to a tiny leather ring around her leg. That kept her in constant contact with him. In case she should try to bolt. In case she should make a sudden rush for freedom and all the good work go to waste.

Archie stepped back as Uncle Craig ducked out the shed door.

He took a deep breath.

There she was! In all her feathered glory!

Free.

Astonished once again, all Archie could do was stare. Two huge plates of yellow for eyes. Mottle plumage, like tortoiseshell. A brilliant snowy Y-shaped band down the face. Butter-coloured legs ending in talons like great fish hooks. And those two tufts of downy feathers rising above the crown of the head. All so soft and glossy and pure. Like nothing else.

Uncle Craig held up the arm which had turned into a perch. The owl's head swivelled one way and then back to stare at Archie. She was studying the forest, her habitat. She was looking right into the small boy before her.

"Struck dumb, then, Little'un?"

"She looks great, Uncle Craig!"

They meandered around the forest trail that took them to higher ground where the big clearing was. That was Uncle Craig's 'Meadow', his circus ring. He went there to look at things – look into things – and meditate. And now perform.

He knelt on one knee and the owl flapped her wings and Archie, too close, was startled and felt a powerful draught.

Uncle Craig made a soothing, clucking kind of noise. "There, there, girl, no need for panic."

Archie watched as Uncle Craig unpicked the owl off his forearm and plopped her onto the piny bracken. Then he unbuckled the gauntlet and handed it to Archie. "Strap it up tight on your arm, same place as I did, just above the wrist."

Archie's heart rattled in his chest. He did as he was told. He felt himself becoming nervous, almost fearful.

The gauntlet was tight. It made him aware of his pulse. He tried to twist the leather: it wouldn't budge. That was perfect.

Uncle Craig silently and slowly handed the leash, all thirty yards of thin powerful line looped like a lariat, to Archie. He whispered. "She needs to be quiet at first, settled, before she lets rip."

Archie swallowed hard. It was that feeling of being on trial.

Uncle Craig said, "Now stand up slowly and lift your arm, gently now, no hurry, and just flick your arm upwards a bit, encourage her, and she'll get the message."

Midmar Forest seemed to hum all around them. The freezing air was pure, still, as if awaiting action.

Archie felt Free's weight but still managed to make a flicking upwards movement with his perch-arm.

The bird's great wings opened and flapped mightily. Archie felt not only a powerful wind but the wing tips crashing against his face. He panicked, groaned, grimaced, turned his head away. He crouched, fearful, losing his nerve.

Uncle Craig grabbed Archie's shoulders and steadied him and pulled him upright. "Now look, now she's going!" he hollered.

And the owl had gone in a whisker. And the leash sang as it played out. And Archie looked back and saw Free thundering around the clearing on a tight line. And he felt the tug on his forearm. And he felt the power and the grace of the bird running through the line and all around his own body like an electric current.

Free flew with amazing speed and power around the invisible circle in the air. At times she ducked to the ground and skimmed against bracken. At times she rose against the blue of the sky. At times she almost touched the trunks of the circle of surrounding pines.

Uncle Craig shouted, "You've done it, Archie! Look at her go! She's accepted you, she loves you, she's showing you what she can do."

Archie could say nothing. It was enough to swivel on his heels and sense the electric power of the owl. She went like lightning, dipping and soaring and straining on the leash. Like a kite with an inbuilt motor.

But then, just for one fleeting moment, Uncle Craig's words – 'She's accepted you, she loves you' – caused an image of his mother to cross his mind. A mental picture of his mother and the female bird blended oddly into one and somehow tugged at his heart. 'She loves you. . .'

It passed quickly and he was elated again, caught up in the moment.

Half an hour later the long-eared owl was restored to her perch in the settled darkness of the garden shed. Uncle Craig gave Archie some dead mice to feed her. Archie hated handling them. But he'd learned much about nature from his uncle and knew that this was the only way: beauty and death together. One thing dies so that another lives.

CHAPTER TWELVE

A Private Chat

Uncle Craig had to drive off somewhere in the Land Rover. Something about a job. He didn't want Archie to go with him, so Archie spent a few hours in the cottage with Aunty Brenda. She wasn't as exciting as his uncle, but she was kind and steady and the meals she made were out of this world. If Uncle Craig was a fast-flowing torrent, then Aunty Brenda was the rock that kept everything anchored.

Aunty Brenda had piled logs on the fire. Archie loved its crackle and hiss. She patted the seat of Uncle Craig's armchair.

"Come on, Archie, park yersel' in your uncle's chair while he's out. It's not often anyone gets the chance to do that!"

Aunty Brenda grinned mischievously. Archie loved seeing the twinkle in her pale blue eyes. He wished he could see the same twinkle in his own mother's. When Rosie was born there had been a twinkle, but then it seemed to vanish and it never came back.

"Archie, we'll have a little heart-to-heart."

"What's that?"

"That's a chat – a private one, no one else to know."

"Oh – about Free?"

"Who?"

Archie chuckled. "The owl, silly!"

Aunty Brenda joined him in laughter. "That and other things."

Archie stared at the burning logs. They made a little cave of bright orange. Every now and then they'd shift as they burnt down and a mass of sparks would fly up the chimney. He loved watching those sparks jiggle like living things.

He loved the peacefulness of the tiny sitting-room at Hirn Lodge.

Aunty Brenda cocked her head at Archie. Her face formed a question mark. "Not got much to say for yersel' this evening. I thought you were full of the owl your uncle trained up for you."

"I am." But Archie's voice was quiet, dreamy; he was entranced by the glow of the log fire which pulsed like a heart.

"You know about your mum, don't you?"

Archie managed to drag his glance away from the fire for once. He stared straight into Aunty Brenda's eyes. "She's going to have another. . .Rosie." He almost said 'baby'.

Aunty Brenda smiled, amused. "Another Rosie?"

"Yes, or maybe the old Rosie'll come back to us. That's what it is."

"Oh." Aunty Brenda didn't know what to say about that. It seemed peculiar: another Rosie, or the same one back again. How could he think in such a way? Then she said, "Well, Archie, your mother needs to get better first. She's trying, you know. She'll beat it. She needs to if the baby. . . the next Rosie, is to be all right."

Matter-of-factly, Archie said, "I know. She's thrown out most of those bottles she had in her room. She's eating a bit now. And she's coming out more often. I saw her take a bottle into her room yesterday, though, after Christmas dinner. Was it wine or just water?"

Aunty Brenda knelt down on the little patchwork carpet in front of the hearth. Wood ash was scattered over the hearth tiles. She got a small brush from the log basket and swept the ash against the grate. Then she turned and looked up at Archie where he sat enclosed by his uncle's huge armchair and said, "She didn't touch a drop of it, Archie. When you went for a walk with your uncle, I went in the backroom to see her. We had a quiet chat, just like this one. She said there were only dregs in the bottom of the bottle anyway. She took it in there out of habit. She handed me the bottle, Archie, and gave me the sweetest smile you could ever wish to see and she swore she'd never touch a drop of the hard stuff again."

Archie said nothing. He stared into the blue of Aunty Brenda's eyes. He knew she never lied.

Something in him soared upwards when he heard those words. The flight of a bird into the sky, a flight for freedom.

Uncle Craig came back late on Boxing Day. Archie had missed his favourite uncle. Aunty Brenda was lovely, but she didn't go out into the forest, she didn't take him to new places or startle him with things.

When Archie got back into Aberdeen he noticed how unusually quiet the streets were. Everyone must be at home enjoying Christmas, eating and drinking and snoozing and trying out new things and watching television.

He wanted to go down to the harbour again. He knew that gulls did not know about Christmas or any other special occasions. He knew that Free would be locked in the darkness of the garden shed. The thought saddened him. The thought of a wild animal held captive, however well it was treated.

But he couldn't hold anything against Uncle Craig. Uncle Craig was his second father. And he, Archie, was his aunt and uncle's son on Friday nights.

Archie stood in the hall, at the foot of the stairs. Suddenly he felt totally alone, as if time had stopped and there was nowhere to go and no one to see and nothing to do but stand alone in the gloom. It was a peculiar feeling which he'd had too often before.

The muffled sound of the television came through a wall. Nothing came from the backroom. He thought he heard gulls shrieking in the distance. He though he heard an owl hooting. But these were imaginings and he knew it.

A dark shadow in the shape of a big bird passed over him. He looked up and saw the jagged ends of wingtips and the fish hooks of talons rise up the staircase wall and float through the upstairs landing. It was peculiar. He felt no fear but allowed the image to linger in his mind.

He went up to his bedroom. It was dim in the dark space. He pulled open the curtains and looked up at the sky. It formed a thick blanket of grey. There was more snow up there. But not a single bird flew.

Archie turned back to the room. In the corner on his chest of drawers sat the new computer that his father had set up for him.

'You can learn everything from that little square screen in the comfort of your own room. Even better than the telly!'

He knew it wasn't true. As young as he was, Archie wasn't so easily fooled. What could you learn about looking after owls, about flying them on a leash, from pictures on a screen? You just sat down and gawped. That's all you did. You had none of the forest smells, the wind in your hair, the rise and fall of your body on tracks and rocks and trees, the wetness of the rain and the blindingness of the snow. You had a flicker instead and diagrams and an artificial voice. It was a dead thing.

Archie remembered the owl handbook that Agnie had given him.

He rummaged around and found it under his bed with socks and shoes and seashells and odd bits of driftwood. He wished he'd looked after it better. It seemed to insult Free to shove a book about her under his bed.

He lay at an angle across the bed with his feet jutting into the air and the book propped open on his pillow. He tried to blot out the mutter of the television and his father's laughter which rose together like a distant storm through the carpet.

He read, 'Owl order. Medium to large birds of prey, usually of nocturnal habits and with round facial discs. Sexes alike. Plumage variegated, often in shades of brown, feathers constructed for silent flapping flight.'

He understood most of that, but a few words puzzled him. Uncle Craig would know. But he'd have to wait a week to find out. He thought of asking his father. But his father only grew irritated when Archie pestered him during a good programme. And then he thought of his mother. He hadn't thought to question her about anything since Rosie had been taken away a whole year ago. A lifetime.

Now was the moment to try. Now, now, when he felt her coming back just a little bit. 'A private chat.' When a new Rosie fluttered somewhere, gradually coming to life, hidden in a nest beyond his imagination.

CHAPTER THIRTEEN

A Miracle

The backroom seemed so distant, as if it was part of another house. Mrs Edgar patted the seat of the chair at the end of her bed. Archie sat in it. The chair smelled of ash and roses and something unpleasantly sharp. He waited for his mother to speak. It was like being in church and she was a priest he didn't know very well.

Mrs Edgar perched on the end of the bed and took one of Archie's hands and rubbed it gently between her own. He remembered her doing that years ago when he'd been out in the snow for hours and his fingers were blue and he came indoors crying because of the pain and she rubbed his fingers hard to make the blood come back and then they went bright red and hurt much more for a bit and she said, 'That's the blood coming and the nerves working. Don't worry, they won't drop off now!' And he had laughed loudly through his tears and saw the world through water and felt a puzzling mixture of misery and joy.

Her rubbing his hand brought it all back.

His mother. His old mam. His lovely angel who always glowed BR: Before Rosie.

"Now, Archie, love, you know I'm trying. I have to now, don't I? And you know why?"

She smiled tenderly. He didn't quite understand his own sadness. "Because Rosie's coming back?"

"Well, sort of. Another sister, shall we say?"

"You promise?" He felt a stab of panic. It might all be a story.

"Promise. But you've got to be good. You've got to start going back to school when the holidays finish."

"I'll do anything, Mam." And he meant it.

She stopped rubbing his hand and he took it back: one hand bone white, the other red as a traffic light.

"Now, Archie, love, there's something on your mind."

So much, he thought, I couldn't begin to tell you. But all he said was, "Words."

"Words? Which words?"

"Variegated. That's one."

Mrs Edgar frowned, thinking. "Don't know that. You'll have to ask your Uncle Craig. He'll know, he's the brainbox of the family."

"What about nocturnal?"

"Oh, that means awake at night, asleep in the day." And she laughed and added, "Like me over the past year!"

Archie stared at his mother's pale, line, changed face. He didn't see the joke.

"How about discs?"

"Discs are circles of anything. Records, CDs and that."

"So facial discs means. . ."

"Round faces. Simple as that. You see, love, I'm not *so* dense."

"Dense?"

"Thick. Stupid. Brainless. This is turning into an English lesson – like the dozens you've missed!"

At last Archie managed a smile.

His mother was teasing, she was coming back. She had put on weight around the middle, although the rest of her was broom-handle thin. In her eyes just the hint of a twinkle, not as clear and bright as Aunty Brenda's. Greenish rather than blue. But something like a lamp burning brighter in her head, its light coming out through her eyes. Like the first touch of dawn.

Archie said, "Mam, when will we have the new baby?"

"Oh, a good few months yet. In spring."

"And what'll we call her?"

"A miracle."

The New Year. No let-up in the bitter weather. Snow had been lying everywhere for weeks. Midmar Forest was a gigantic pure white quilt punctured by the needles of pine trees. Aberdeen seemed almost to have been abandoned to the gulls and gritting lorries.

A knock at the front door.

It couldn't be the postman or the milkman on New Year's Day. It might be a surprise visit from Uncle Craig and Aunty Brenda.

Archie's father never heard the doorbell or even mad thumping against the wooden panels because the television was so loud. And his mother never bothered to leave the backroom except to go to the bathroom or the kitchen, or to put empties out in the yard.

Archie leapt down the stairs three at a time.

The door knocking became louder. Whoever it was didn't bother to stab at the bell press.

Archie flung the door wide open and stared skywards. Uncle Craig's face didn't appear high above him. All that was there was cloud.

But lower down, near the ground, Agnie Robson's face hovered, smiling and cold – like a pale disc.

"Hello, Archie. What did you get for Christmas?"

The question took him by surprise. So did she, standing there: Agnie Robson.

"Not much."

"I got a loada CDs and DVDs and clothes and…"

"Why've you come today? It's New Year's Day, Ag. People don't. . ."

"I was bored, Arch. I've played all the CDs and DVDs – twice. And I've tried on all the clothes – six times. And all the trifle's gone. And the sausage rolls."

"And. . .?"

"And I want to show you the Den."

"The what?"

"The Den. Remember I mentioned it, ages ago?"

"No."

"Top secret place. In St Kilda's Church."

Archie went cold, colder than standing at the door with more snow threatening. "You want me to go to church?"

Agnie laughed. "No stupid! Not 'go to church', not like that. It's a ruin and our camp's there and when all the gang from school get bored at home they go to St Kilda's – the church, the Den."

"And what do they do there?"

Agnie lifted her eyes to heaven, just like a parent who can't believe their child's stupidity. "Play! Plan things! Swap cards and mags and CDs! Catch creepy crawlies and do things."

"Do things?"

"Come on, I'll show you."

"I can't – it's New Year's Day."

"You can. Step out the door and use your legs. It's easy."

Archie shouted to his father about going out awhile. Without shifting his eyes from the comedy show, Dodie Edgar yelled, "Okay, lad! But wrap up warm and get back before dark. Great film on tonight. You'll wanna see it wi' me. You see."

Archie walked down the street with Agnie. It felt so strange. Awful Agnie strolled by his side. Agnie his sworn enemy. Agnie who stuck up for him in class. The only one who *might* have appreciated the owl talk.

"Where are we going, Ag?"

"I told you – to church."

She giggled when she said that. It sounded silly.

"Is it down here?"

"Down here and left, across the roundabout, straight on, third right, then left, then the other side of the park."

"Oh, *that* church. I thought it was a house now."

"St Kilda's? Not yet. It's still a ruin."

Archie couldn't believe the speed of Agnie's walking. The further they went, the faster she walked. He had to do little runs to keep catching up.

When they reached St Kilda's it seemed to be deserted. A fine coating of snow covered every stone, and the broken spire, and the slates of the roof. Some slates were missing, walls had great holes punched in them where stained glass had been, and the main door was completely missing.

Archie said, "It looks like a bomb's hit it. Ten bombs."

"Come on, it's great!" And Agnie flew through and big stone arch where the door once stood, leaving Archie standing in icy wonder.

He began shivering. He wished he'd stayed at home.

Agnie poked her head out the door and waved him in and hollered, "Come on!"

Inside the main part of St Kilda's – the nave – broken mosaic lay everywhere like glittery gravel. In one corner Archie saw a huge tarpaulin stretched across pillars of piled up stone. Like a teepee in the wrong location.

"What's that?"

"That's the Den. Come on Arch."

Agnie ducked under the tarpaulin. Archie followed. It was surprisingly warm and nest-like, but shadowy and jagged with broken objects.

Archie caught sight of two boys and a girl squatting in one corner. He recognised them from St Bride's, his primary school. St Kilda's and St Bride's: there were so many saints around, which was at least better than devils. Some of the devils teased him, the ones he couldn't shake off.

One boy shouted, "Archie Edgar!"

The others followed suit. "What are *you* doing here?"

The girl said, "He disnae mind coming here, this is the Den, not the school. No lessons, eh?"

Agnie frowned at them. "Leave him alone. I invited him here. Archie's okay."

The children smiled slyly at each other but said nothing more.

All five squatted under the tarpaulin. An arctic draught flew up Archie's trouser legs and made him shiver uncontrollably. He decided it was not fun at all. He remembered why he didn't play out with other children: they just sat around doing silly things or nothing much at all. Getting cold.

Boy One produced a squat glass jar with the lid screwed tight. The lid was punctured with air holes.

Archie said, "What's that?"

Boy Two laughed and said, "A jam jar, stupid!"

Archie said, "I know that."

"Well, why ask?"

"What's in it?"

Boy One lifted the jar in the gloom and said, "Creepy crawlies. Dozens of them."

Archie stared hard but in the darkness saw only the glint of glass. He said, "Why have you got them in there?"

Boy Two said, "Experiments."

"What?"

Agnie chipped in. "He means like you do in class. Science. 'Practical work' Miss Lewis calls it. See what happens and write it down, only we don't write it."

Archie became uneasy. He stared at the dark mass inside the jam jar. Things moved. He didn't want to know any more. He thought of Free sitting in the darkness of the garden shed. Right now. Big golden eyes staring.

'Experiments'. It's what human beings were always doing with animals. It told you new things. But it didn't do the animals much good. They'd rather be left in peace. That's common sense.

Boy Two snatched the glass jar from Boy One. He'd noticed the odd look on Archie's face, as if he would tell someone, as if he would go home and blurt out what he knew about the Den.

Boy Two hid the creepy crawly jar under some scraps of spare tarpaulin. Archie continued to stare at the place for many minutes. He wondered what exactly was trapped in the jar, and what the 'experiments' were.

Agnie said, "Do you like it here, arch?"

Archie didn't know what to reply. All three laughed. They knew he felt strange, lost, a little bit on edge. They could tell from the way he fidgeted. It was another 'experiment': a boy in a peculiar place.

Boy One suddenly came out with it: "Your mam's having another bairn, isn't she?"

An electric shock sliced right through Archie. He almost fell sideways. It was true, but it hit him like a brick. Coming out with it like that.

Agnie said, "Don't be rude, Jamie!"

Boy Two said, "True, though, isn't it? Me Mam told us. She knows. Everyone knows."

Archie thought, 'Everyone?' The whole world? He felt that he couldn't breathe. He felt the tarpaulin press on his head like the wings of a giant black bat.

He said, "I think so." He knew she was due to have another child, a new Rosie, but found himself just saying, "I think so." As if to cast doubt.

The two boys screamed with laughter.

"He thinks so!"

"He doesn't know!"

"His own mammy and he doesn't know!"

The boys shuffled about the Den and stamped with cruel amusement and Archie heard the jam jar smash beneath a scrap of tarpaulin.

Agnie groaned. "Now look what you've done!" All four argued, even the sheepish girl.

Archie took the opportunity.

He ducked out the Den and scooted across the shattered mosaic and out the stone arch where the door had been and ran at full pelt the way he'd come and sucked the crisp cold air into his lungs and his horror turned to relief at the freedom of the bright skies and the sight of gulls wheeling over the harbour in the distance.

When he reached home his instinct took over. Instead of racing up the stairs to his bedroom, he burst into the backroom and flew into his mother's arms as she sat dozing in her bedside chair.

Empties flew everywhere.

CHAPTER FOURTEEN

New Term, New Leaf

Archie lay across his bed with his special notepad open. He garrotted his finger with the elasticated clasp. Ouch!

Every Sunday morning at ten he heard distant church bells, but he knew it couldn't be the bells of St Kilda's.

He began writing:

Dear Rory,

I'm sorry I haven't written for such a long time. Lots bin happening over Christmas. Now I'm catching up. The world is still upside down. When isnt it?

You must be cold and miserable trapped in your tree through the winter. If I could free you I wood, but there are so many trees and I dont know which one you are stuck inside. I could be serching forever. I think your down south somwhere. I imagin you really strongly. My ownly true frend. I dont care if you're a lowlander insted of a highlander.

I dont know why I'm goin on like this.

On Christmas eve there was a nock at the door. I thought it was Ace comin to fetch me, but it was Pain. She messed around a bit then gave me a present. It was a book abowt owls. I dont know why she did that. It mus be to make me feel gilty for all the times I said I hate her. I _do_ feel gilty, Rory. It isnt rite, is it.

When we had Christmas dinner it was aweful. Number One cam out of her room and sat at the table with Number Two and Ace and Angel and me. Number One looked sad. I cept watching her. They all talked about things I couldny understand, like it was a secret langage. But Number One just stared at the walls and I couldny see any light in her eyes, just a mist like.

They all dozed and I went to my room and layed there and the new computer sat there dumb and Ace cam up and suprised me. We walked down to the harbour and I had the feeling he must by my reel dad. It felt great and creepy all at once. Seagulls flew everywere. They bombed us. It was exiting. I didnt mind the cold becos Ace promised he'd take me to see Free the next day, boxing day. He always keeps his promises.

Ace showed me Free again. I cant belive how beautiful owls look. She's kind of prowd and peaceful at the same time. She looks at you and seems to know you. Wise owl like Ace. And gentle like the babe in a manger.

I flew her on the leesh for the first time. Rory, I was so excited, I cant tell you how I felt. I loved it and I love Free, but it made me think of Number One and Rosie (I cant give her any other name) and I remembered what Ace said, that all things live and die and you cant do a thing about it but the Good Book makes it all sound rite and I shood study it one day. I don't know about that, I just have these feelings.

When I was readin the owl book Pain gave me it made me think of the new Rosie, the one thats comin. I dont know why. I always put pictures together in my head like that. My brain must be a very strange thing. How can that thing work. It seems that what I fell in my heart goes straight to my head and my brain makes pictures of it and somtimes the pictures overlap and get me confused, like in dreams. You cant work yourself out, can you, Rory. It's a mistery where it all comes from.

Pain called again. I just wanted her to go away but I remembered the lovly present and felt sorry for her so I went with her to saint Kildas church. It's quite a way. It's a ruin now, God mustve left it. The kids from Miss Lewis class have a camp inside. They call it the Den. Jamie and Rufus were horrible cruel and nasty. They had tiny creechures traped in a glass jar, for experiments. They teesed me and got exited and the jar, broke and I'm glad about that. Let the creechures live.

I excaped out the church door and ran home and straight to Number One and roared like a bairn and she was so shocked. I dont know why I'm tellin you all this, Rory. It wont keep up your spirits but it helps me. You're a reel lissener. I can trust you.

Love, Archie

First day of the new term.

When Archie walked into the classroom, everyone stared. They didn't expect his first appearance until much later in the term, once the Education Welfare Officer had called at his house, about three times. But he wanted to keep his promise.

Miss Lewis beamed. "Archie Edgar! New term, new leaf, eh?"

Archie looked shy, keeping his face lowered. "Yes, Miss."

Rufus grinned. "Found your way here, then, Edgar."

Jamie clapped a hand across his sudden chuckle. "New boy in the class, Miss!"

Agnie Robson frowned. "Shut up, all of you. Give Archie a chance."

Miss Lewis held up both hands and then slowly lowered them, as if putting the lid on a great deal of silly commotion. "We'll have none of that, boys. Welcome Archie back. Where are your manners? Let's all begin the way we mean to continue, class."

Agnie heard the boy in front mutter, "We are, Miss, don't worry." She kicked him and he turned round and widened his eyes like a devil and snarled. Agnie wasn't afraid of any of them.

The morning flew by. Archie stuck close to Agnie, even though a part of him resented her. He kept thinking of the Owl Handbook. He kept thinking of the way she supported him: he wondered why. Why do people take on the role of protectors when no one asks them or pays them?

That morning, during maths and English and science, Archie became aware of a great dark shadow of outstretched wings slowly beating across the classroom. He glanced up every now and then at the ceiling. No one else seemed aware of it. Did the shadow exist only for him?

He pictured Free in his uncle's garden shed: she was flapping in a panic, hungry and alone. She wanted to be outside in the clean clear air. That was the reason for the gigantic shadow that seemed to melt into the fabric of the school building, he told himself. A thrill shot through Archie's body; it was almost a pain, a torment.

After lunch Miss Lewis assembled the children and clapped her hands and announced 'News Time'. They had a brief session every week: how was your weekend? Did you go anywhere, have a party, receive a gift, experience something for the first time in your life? What have you brought to show us?

Miss Lewis lifted her captain's chair into the broken point of the circle. Children always jostled to sit closest to her. Archie felt uncomfortable with crossed legs. He made sure Agnie was close by him; in the uncertainty of the classroom she gave him something to cling on to. But it wasn't like before Christmas when he felt as feeble and frightened as a mouse. This time Archie felt prepared. Things were changing. He felt it in his bones, his heart, and that gave him amazing strength.

Miss Lewis began: "I believe that Archie Edgar has a few important things to tell us all."

A thread of electricity shot through Archie's body. He didn't expect to be called upon quite so soon. First off! It wasn't fair – but then nothing was.

He lifted his lowered head and ran his eyes around the circle. When they came to a halt on Agnie, sitting next to him, she was smiling almost proudly. She leaned towards him and whispered, "Come on, Archie, you can do it."

"Well, Miss. . ." He felt a bone stick in his throat.

Miss Lewis smiled patiently. "Yes, Archie?"

The circle of pupils were nudging each other, trying not to giggle, trying to give Archie a chance because they'd been warned to.

"Well, Miss, I flew Free for the first time ever. . ."

"Free?" Miss Lewis wanted everyone to understand.

"Oh, that's the name of my owl. She's a long-eared owl and she's beautiful. My Uncle Craig keeps her in the garden shed where he lives."

"And where's that, Archie?"

Archie frowned, puzzled; the name of the place escaped him. "In a forest, Miss."

"Okay."

"Well, Miss, I flew Free in the Meadow, first time for me. She was on a leash. . . ."

"That's a kind of long line, like a dog-lead, children."

"But she was so powerful, she nearly pulled me over." The pupils tittered. "Next time I fly her it'll be off the leash so she flies away over the trees and when I call she'll come back and sit on my gauntlet. . ."

One girl called out, "What's a gauntlet?"

Miss Lewis answered, "A big thick leather glove, Susie. It's for protection."

Rufus pointedly asked, "What if she don't come back, Edgar?"

There was a sudden hush, like a big in-drawing of breath. Everyone stared at Archie. The words rattled around in his head: 'What if she don't come back? What if. . .' He couldn't help thinking of new-born Rosie in the snow a year ago. One sight of her at home, and then. . . gone for good. 'What if she don't come back?'

Archie took a deep breath and lifted his shoulders. "She will."

Miss Lewis asked him, "Is that your news, Archie?"

"There's one more thing, Miss."

"Go on, then."

"Me Mam's having another baby."

Shock waves pulsed across the classroom. Children smiled and glanced at each other as if to titter again, as if Archie had said something rude, but Agnie Robson put a finger to her lips and nodded her head up and down like a bossy actress and they remained silent.

Miss Lewis thanked Archie for his news. To his amazement he even got a round of applause. The rest of the school day went like a dream.

CHAPTER FIFTEEN

'What if she don't come back?'

Archie could hardly sleep at all on Friday night in his aunt and uncle's cottage. He'd been promised his first flight off the leash with Free early the next morning. Uncle Craig had taught him the peculiar whistle that would turn the owl in flight and bring her back. He'd been practising it. He'd been whistling in the darkness of the little spare bedroom and he couldn't get to sleep. He'd been imagining Free soaring above the forest pines and circling further away and then getting lost. A stone seemed to drop right through his body. The stone reminded him of other things at home in the backroom: the empty bottles, the changing look of his mother, the time to come. At least, this time, there wouldn't be snow.

Uncle Craig said, "Here we go, then."

They had reached the Meadow. All around them pine trees sang in the wind. You could smell salt off the faraway sea.

Uncle Craig slipped the gauntlet off gently with Free perched on it, her talons biting into the leather. She swivelled her head; she seemed calm. The wind lifted her breast feathers and showed white under tortoise-shell. She seemed to know what was about to happen: wise owl.

Archie held his left arm out straight. Uncle Craig jiggled the gauntlet over his hand. Free wobbled as the gauntlet moved, but still she seemed content. The owl's wing touched Archie's cheek as he held her – it made him shiver, not with cold but with a kind of inner joy.

Uncle Craig whispered, "Okay, Archie, now unclip the leash; gently now, the way I showed you."

Archie felt the tin drum of his heart.

He unclipped the leash from the jesses. Free stared at him with those magnificent amber eyes. There was still the fierceness of the wild in them.

"She's free now," Archie said. He was jangling with nerves. A boy's voice rattled in his head: 'What if she don't come back?'

"Now raise your arm, Little'un. Give it a quick flick and she'll be off."

Archie daren't. She'd never return. She was wild, she'd find her brothers and sisters and that would be it.

But he flicked his perch-arm upwards.

A great flutter of wings beat about his face.

When he opened his eyes the owl was flapping like crazy, rising, rising to the height of the pines, clearing the Meadow.

"There she goes, Little'un!" Uncle Craig's voice shrilled.

Archie stood in shocked wonder. He couldn't utter a sound. He stared at Free as she swooped this way and that and diminished in size and cleared the topmost branch of the tallest pine. Then he heard himself yelling, "She won't come back! Uncle Craig, she's gone, she won't come back!"

Archie's uncle knelt down on the bracken and clutched his nephew's shoulders reassuringly and put his head close to Archie's and said, "Steady, steady, Little'un, no need to panic. She'll stretch her wings and explore the territory – they always do that – and then she'll return. You see."

Archie stood with his uncle, dead centre of the Meadow. They craned their heads around the battlements of the pine tops. All that could be heard was the whipping of the stiff wind. There was a terrible absence of birdsong and wing beating.

"Okay, Archie, cluck your tongue and give it a whistle, just like I taught you."

Archie tried it: a cluck and a whistle.

He watched and waited. The sky remained empty. He felt the empty tin of his heart rattle with a single pebble. It wasn't empty. But it hurt. Uncle Craig said nothing. Archie knew it had been a mistake. Free was a wild bird, her training only a temporary thing. She must feel the pull of the forest. It was stronger than anything.

And then he saw her again.

That unmistakeable blur of orange and brown rising above the pine tops, beating down on the two human figures.

"Raise your gauntlet, Archie. Quick!"

Archie raised his left arm high. The owl came suddenly, pulling in her wings and plummeting like a stone. She crashed down onto the gauntlet.

"She's back! She's back!"

Archie couldn't contain himself. He jumped up and down madly.

It was as if something had died and then been born again.

Aunty Brenda had made a Victoria sponge. It sat on the kitchen table. The dusting of icing sugar on the top looked like fine snow. Archie adored the home-made strawberry filling. Aunty Brenda bought masses of Kentish strawberries every July and ate some fresh and then froze the rest.

Aunty Brenda busied herself in the kitchen, something she loved to do, whilst Uncle Craig and Archie sat in the matching armchairs pulled up close to the log fire. Archie's favourite trick was to rest his stockinged heels on the hearth surround and slowly toast the soles of his feet. Sometimes, if he'd been out in the forest with his uncle and the moisture had got through to his socks, he could see evaporation rising from the toes of his socks and he'd remark to Uncle Craig, "Look, my toes are on fire!" and his uncle would always reply, "Better toss them on the big burn, then, they're no good to you now!"

It always went like that. Archie loved the regular routine: Friday nights, Midmar Forest, fish supper, the cosy spare room, Aunty's Saturday breakfast, a walk through the pines to the Meadow, back for lunch, the Land Rover ride into Aberdeen, afternoon football.

He knew it would have to change, though.

Archie stared at two crossed logs crackling in the flames.

Uncle Craig shoved a huge piece of Victoria sandwich into his mouth, almost crunching his fork in two.

"Your Aunty feeds me too well, Little'un."

Archie didn't reply; he was thinking of something else.

The fire glow in the darkened room made him think things that were sad but also beautiful.

"Do you think Free is happy locked in the shed, Uncle?"

"For now, yes."

"But not forever."

"No, 'course not. She'll have to be given her liberty."

Archie looked across at his uncle, who was pushing crumbs into his mouth from the corners of his lips. He seemed to be pigging himself.

"I know when to release her into the world, Uncle."

"You do? And when might that be?"

"When the baby's born."

Uncle Craig smiled tenderly at Archie. "You're a big softie!"

"And you're a pig, Uncle. All that cake'll make you sick!"

"You young. . ." Uncle Craig leaned out of the armchair and grabbed Archie's ankle. Archie squealed and called for his aunty to rescue him. She rushed in from the kitchen, wiping soapy hands down her apron. "What's all this commotion?"

"Leave us, Bren, go back to your beloved baking. Archie's being very rude to his favourite uncle."

Aunty Brenda smiled and looked up at the ceiling as if to say, 'Look at those two silly young bairns.'

Archie loved the undivided attention he got from Uncle Craig. He asked, "Do you think Free knows what'll happen to her?"

"What an odd question!"

"Do you, Uncle Craig?"

"Happen to her? No. You see, animals live completely in the present, unlike we poor human beings."

"What do you mean?"

"How can I put it?" Uncle Craig fingered the last few crumbs of sponge and put his plate on the flickering hearth. He scratched his head. Archie sat in the huge armchair and seemed to disappear. "We're always worrying about what'll happen tomorrow, next week, next year. And we're always revisiting the past: could I have done this or that differently? Because we're so concerned about the past and the future, the present flies by and we hardly even notice it. Animals, including owls, aren't like that. A pain comes and goes and is forgotten. Sometimes it's better not to have much of a memory! It gets you into a real tizz. Animals live by their instincts,

72

Little'un. Their whole world is the world of the present, what's happening *now*. So, no, Free won't have a clue about what's going to happen to her. And she'll be the happier for it!"

Archie thought he understood, but on balance decided it was better to recall the past and anticipate the future, and maybe live for the moment as well. Couldn't you do all three things?

"Do you get it, Little'un?"

"I think so."

Uncle Craig smiled and his face became a strange patchwork of shadows in the glow of the logs.

"It's late. Come on – bed. You've kept me up talking late as usual."

"No, Uncle Craig, you've kept *me* up!"

CHAPTER SIXTEEN

Eggs and Bacon

When Archie woke on Sunday morning he couldn't hear the television. An eerie silence enveloped him. Usually Dodie Edgar was up very early – more accurately dozing on the sofa – watching some breakfast news on the box. This silence reminded Archie of Hirn Lodge, and yet he was in the middle of Aberdeen.

Soon there came the lone cry of a gull. Archie found himself smiling under the duvet. There was such sadness in a gull's cry, and yet it brought a deep thrill. One bird reminded him of another. He pictured endless ocean, endless forest, endlessness itself. Doesn't the whole world go on like that until it meets itself and completes the circle?

The lone gull must have fled its chimney stack. Silence expanded again. Why no telly? He didn't much like it but had grown to regard it as normal.

Archie crept downstairs in his pyjamas. It was freezing. He pulled the top tight across his chest.

The sitting room door was ajar. He pushed it slowly. There was no bluish glare from the television. He felt nervous, the tin drum in his chest rattling. When the door swung wide open, Archie saw his mother sitting neatly at one end of the sofa where his father usually sprawled. As if she were a sculpted bookend.

He was amazed. "Mam!"

She turned, but slowly, without energy or surprise. "Archie, what are you doing up so early?"

"I didn't hear Dad's telly; I usually hear it in my sleep."

Mollie Edgar patted the cushion next to her. "Come and sit here, love."

Archie sat alongside his mother and she hugged him close. The sitting room felt so different without the television's boom and glare. It had calmed down.

"Are you all right, Mam? Why are you in here all on your own?"

"Oh, I'm fed up with the backroom." She laughed as she added, "Thought I'd explore the world!"

Archie noticed how his mother's stomach had begun to bulge just a little. The rest of her was so thin that her middle stood out. He looked at the floor around her slippered feet for signs of a bottle. There was nothing but a carpet littered with crisp fragments.

Mollie Edgar said "Put your hand there, Arch."

She took his hand and placed it over her stomach. In the silence he concentrated hard.

"Feel anything?"

He yearned to say, 'Yes, the next Rosie', but he felt nothing except a kind of deep warmth. "I'm not sure, Mam." It was not so much a physical sensation as a vision that came to him: the owl's nest at the base of a pine. Five pure white eggs. His uncle's voice: You have to watch very slowly and always listen. Or they vanish. Secret of life.

He didn't want Rosie to vanish. That happened last winter. Something precious goes and it never returns. Flies off. You can't keep everything on a leash. Some creatures are born wild and stay wild. All need a mother's love.

Archie took his hand away from his mother's stomach. "It's Rosie, isn't it?"

"Sort of, Archie. Another version, if you like. Mark Two. But we'll see."

"Why isn't Dad here?"

"He had to go off early, meet your uncle. Something about a new job. About time, eh? With another bairn to feed we'll need every penny."

The smile on his mother's face, pale and thin as it was, warmed Archie.

He lay on his bed, his notebook with its elasticated clasp in front of him. He wanted to write a quick note to Rory, but for the first time nothing much would come to mind. He chewed the pencil end and swung his legs in the air like a crazy windmill. Why could he not put any words down?

Then the gorgeous smell twitched his nostrils.

He assumed it came from next door, even though his window was closed. Through the wall. Strong smells can penetrate walls. Not a bad smell, though. Quite the opposite. Something delicious that not only twitched his nostrils but his stomach too.

Eggs and bacon!

It was unmistakeable.

Archie felt the saliva gather in his mouth. What an amazing effect an odour can have! His whole body reacted. This must be what happens to creatures living in the present.

He rushed downstairs and the smell became overwhelming. He felt almost sick for a taste of eggs and bacon. Food can turn you manic. That's why animals fight over it.

The kitchen drew him like a magnet.

He went in and saw his mother jiggling the big silver frying pan on the cooker. She was turning the bacon with a spatula and dripping fat on the sizzling eggs.

"Mam, what are you doing?"

Without turning, because she had to concentrate, Mollie Edgar replied, "It's Sunday morning, Arch. Remember what I used to do in the old days?"

In a slow tone of wonder, Archie said, "Sunday fry-up."

"Correct!"

"But you haven't done that for. . ."

"Don't tell me: over a year. I know. About time I did, then. There's enough for you, me and your Dad. I'm sick of eatin' sandwiches and drinkin' poison in the backroom. Besides, I've got to eat and drink for two now."

Archie sat at the breakfast table with his mother. He could hardly recall the last time he'd done that. It must have been before Rosie came and went.

Eggs and bacon had never tasted so good.

Agnie Robson hadn't called round. Archie wondered if she would. He told himself he didn't want her to – she was a pain. And yet, a little piece of him, somewhere in the background, wanted her friendship. He told himself repeatedly that he didn't need any other friend than the long-eared owl. But the owl would have to be released when winter turned into spring and summer was tipping Scotland over the edge into something a little warmer. You couldn't keep a bird as a long-term friend. His owl needed to be, as the name suggested, 'free'.

And Rory?

Well, Rory was trapped inside a tree and Archie didn't know where exactly and anyway it was only possible to write letters and yearn and imagine. He recalled how Miss Lewis had explained to the class about Ann Frank's diary-friend, about what comfort she had brought in wartime, about the fact that her friend could never just turn up at the door.

Imagination is amazing, Miss Lewis had said, but it only goes so far – then you are left with the real world with all its sores and warts and cuts and bruises. And its touchable beauty. Its *real*ness.

Archie was pleased that Agnie had not called round. It meant he could wend his way through the back streets to the ruin of St Kilda's Church and explore the Den on his own. If the boys were not there. If the demolition gang were not already swinging their giant ball and chain at its walls.

He stepped through the curved stone arch where the door had once swung on its black hinges. The hinges were still embedded in one wall: a history lesson.

The Den looked completely empty, its tarpaulin limp, its entrance a hole like an open mouth. Archie crunched over broken masonry and fragments of stained glass and tiny pieces of mosaic flooring. He wondered how a house of God could be left in such a state.

He imagined the people who had once worshipped here, the wooden pews, the altar with lit candles, maybe tapestries and effigies and beautiful carved screens. All gone, all crumbled to dust or stolen and used in other places. What must God think, looking down on this? Like a great creative bird viewing its plundered nest from the sky. Its eggs were the church's many scattered objects.

Archie ducked into the mouth of the Den. Only enough light penetrated to see shadows. He scrambled out again and peeled the tarpaulin back. Everything was revealed. He knew that Agnie and the gang would not thank him for this.

There were all sorts of objects scattered about the cracked tile floor. It was like a magpie's nest – shiny little things stolen from everywhere. He noticed the broken glass of the jam jar. A meandering trail of dead insects led from the broken glass. He wished they had been able to get away before they'd died in the jar.

Jamie and Rufus were cruel: you can trap a creature, keep it for a while, feed it, study it, treat it with kindness – but then you should let it return to its natural habitat. How else can the world work properly? But no, not them, they wanted to control and then 'experiment' and that led to death. Adults do that.

Archie shuffled his feet amongst the Den's confused mass of objects. They made a sound like breaking waves crunching on shingle. The Den looked cheerier with its tarpaulin roof half pulled back. He wondered whether the gang would suddenly turn up and yell at him and attack him. He didn't feel bothered.

Then he caught sight of the skeleton.

In one corner, tucked away, was the whole and perfect skeleton of a bird. It had been carefully placed on an unbroken bright red tile. It seemed like an offering. Agnie or one of the others must have found it. She once said to him that people worship funny things and he hadn't known what she was getting at.

Archie went over to the spot where the bird skeleton lay. He crouched down to get a better look. He daren't touch it. Something about it kept him at bay. But he stared in fascination.

He couldn't tell what kind of bird it was. It was clearly on its back, its tiny skull perfect, its legs and claws curled up. Its wings were like fine lace.

Archie thought of Free, and a great wave of sadness swept through him. Then he thought of Rosie buried under deep snow. What had become of her? Then he thought of the Rosie-to-come and felt himself break into a tiny smile.

Whenever something dies, something else is born. He found himself full of such thoughts.

CHAPTER SEVENTEEN

Gurgling Sounds

"I can till smell a powerful pong of fry-up in here, son."

Dodie Edgar crouched at the cooker trying to clean off the grease with a scourer. Archie sat at the table, a bowl and a carton of milk and a box of Krispies in front of him. It all seemed a million miles from Midmar Forest.

"Yesterday was the best breakfast I've had in a whole year," Archie declared.

"That's as mebbe, son, but it's back to Krispies today – and then school. You promised your mother."

"Yes, Dad. But I'm not sure about school. . ."

Dodie Edgar stopped attacking the cooker with the scourer. He turned and looked up at his son. "Not sure? What do you mean, 'not sure'?"

Archie's face took on a thoughtful, twisted look. "I mean, you just sit there at a desk with all the others and you read things and fill up books with words and answers and pictures and. . ."

Dodie Edgar intervened. "And what? What else do you expect to do, son?"

"It doesn't seem right way to learn about things, Dad."

"Didn't do me any harm when I was at school."

"Yes, Dad – but did it do you any good?"

Archie's father scratched his nose with the scourer. Good question. He looked down at the bare floorboards and frowned and seemed stumped for once. Then the answer came.

"But every kid goes to school, Arch."

"Do they, Dad? I heard about some that don't."

"That was in the old days."

"No, now, today."

"They must be home-schooled kids." He broke into a mischievous smile. "And you, Archie Edgar!"

Archie spooned Krispies into his mouth. He didn't laugh; he didn't take the bait. He insisted on being serious.

"But you learn by *doing*, Dad, not reading."

"What?"

"I'm thinking of Uncle Craig training Free."

"Who?"

"Free – my owl."

"Oh."

"He did it by *doing* it, not by reading about it. And he showed me how to do it, out there in the forest. You couldn't do that in a classroom, could you?"

Dodie Edgar seemed to forget about scouring the cooker free of grease. Archie had a point, but his father needed to put him straight.

"That's all very well, son, but certain things have to be done in the peace and quiet of a classroom, with a teacher."

"Peace and quiet, Dad? You should hear them!"

"Well, yeah, it isn't ideal. But maths, for instance, or history – you gotta work things out and know the facts."

"But, but. . ."

"Come on, Archie Edgar, get those Krispies down yer throat and get yerself organised for school! And let me get this smelly cooker clean! There's eggs and bacon crawling all over it!"

Archie didn't want to talk about school when he got home. Besides, his father was sprawled on the sofa in the sitting room with the television blaring and his laughter threatening to shake the house down.

You couldn't get through to him then. If there was a comedy show on the box he wouldn't take anything seriously. The world could explode and he'd die laughing. That was Dodie Edgar. He'd been like it since the oil rigs shut down and he'd lost his job and found himself twiddling his thumbs. Now his thumbs twiddled the remote.

Archie tapped lightly on the door of the backroom. All day at school he'd been thinking about his mother's hospital visit. What did they do there? Hospitals sent Archie cold. Rosie had gone to one a year ago and not come out.

He heard his mother's voice. Instead of the usual dull moan it sounded bright and cheerful. "Come in, Arch, love, I know it's you."

"How?"

"That soft little knock. Your father hammers and just bursts in!"

Archie saw his mother sitting in her armchair at the foot of the bed.

"I went to school, Mam."

"I know. What was it like?"

Archie pulled a face. "Oh, it was all right. . ."

"Be honest, Arch."

"It was horrible."

Mollie Edgar held her arms out to Archie and he came over to her chair and she hugged him close. "Whatever are we going to do with you?"

"Let me live in the forest near Uncle Craig and *that* can be my school."

Mollie Edgar tousled her son's hair and smiled. "On your own? What could you teach yourself there?"

"Everything about owls."

"Owls? That's not all there is in life, Arch. You've got to learn about the world, get yourself set up in a career and all that kind of stuff. I know you're much too young yet, but. . ."

"But we can *all* live there, Mam."

"All?"

"You, me, Dad and the new Rosie. Have our own little school, like."

Archie sounded so excited, as if it could really happen: two mothers, two fathers, a baby sister and all the creatures you could want on your doorstep. A gigantic outdoor classroom. The mere thought shot a thrill through him.

Mollie Edgar had been holding Archie tightly against her while they spoke. She did not want to let him go. She had let him go twelve months before and taken to the bottle and turned her face away from the world. It had been a seeping poison. But now things were different. Now she had emptied all the poison away. She held

81

him even closer, afraid suddenly that if she let go he might take flight like that owl he was always talking about. He was not on a leash, except perhaps the invisible kind of leash which always ties a mother to her child.

"Mam?"

"Yes, Archie?"

"I can feel something."

"What?"

The side of his face was clasped against her bulging stomach.

"What can you feel?"

"Something moving about. And I can hear things."

"What can you hear?"

"Gurgling sounds. Is that you or the new Rosie?"

Mollie Edgar laughed gently, almost sadly. "That's the both of us, I think. Must be. We're like one until the baby's born."

Suddenly Archie pulled free from his mother's grip and stood up and displayed the warmest smile she could remember.

"Mam, I want you to see Free."

"Who?"

"Free – it's the name I gave to the long-eared owl that Uncle Craig keeps for me."

"Oh. Well. . ."

"I'll ask him to drive us all into the forest when he comes on Friday. He won't mind. Would you like that, Mam, would you?"

Mollie Edgar felt tired and achy. She hadn't been to her sister's house in well over a year. The thought of travelling out of Aberdeen itself horrified her. She stared long at Archie. He was awaiting her reply, a fixed expectant grin on his face. How could you disappoint a son?

"If you can persuade your uncle, I'll come. But I'm not sure your father could drag himself away from that blabbin' television for more than a few hours. He's got to think about his new job."

Archie almost exploded with joy. "Oh, Mam, Mam!"

CHAPTER EIGHTEEN

Studying Clouds

February spilled over into March. Aberdeenshire lay iron hard in the grip of frosts and snow flurries. They would come and go for months yet before there was any prospect of real warmth.

To the west of Aberdeen, the further you went from the coast, the colder and wilder it got. Loch of Skene's waters still showed a shiny skin of ice across its length and breadth. Surrounding pine forests were tinged with white and stood defiant and frozen. It was hard to imagine anything like summer.

The chimneys of lodges and cottages sent up twisting plumes of smoke from cosy fires. To the south, Drum Castle lay in a magical mist. To the north-west, Castle Fraser sat on the hills like a pale phantom. All the burns were frozen. The A944 road from Aberdeen west to Alford was treacherous with ice and fog. And Cullerlie Stone Circle, where Archie's uncle had promised to take him, stood like a ring of giant's dice thrown over the iron hard igneous rock.

It was not a time to be outdoors unless you loved it, unless you were tough enough to ignore the intense cold. It was a time when many Scots dream of the southerly sun, of escape from the greyness and the granite and the overheated indoors. It was a time for watching for signs of spring's miraculous birth.

But some loved it. Some, like Uncle Craig, were born to it and wanted to show others the beauties of a cold hard needle-sharp climate. Foresters and gillies and stone builders scoffed at the softies down south, but always gently, without any malice. They knew the southerners come up here for the islands, lochs and mountains and the special atmosphere you seemed to get nowhere else in the Kingdom. It wasn't any more porridge or haggis or bagpipes than

London was jellied eels or France was horsemeat. You saw what you wanted to see and ate whatever pleased you. But you always made sure you wrapped up warm.

Mollie Edgar wrapped up warm for the ride west to Midmar Forest. She had hardly left the backroom in a year, let alone the house, let alone Aberdeen. She had almost forgotten how chilling a Scottish spring could be. Despite the growing brightness in the sky, you didn't take liberties. Climbers and walkers knew that.

Aunty Brenda was busy with the fish supper; this time she had to set an extra two places. The batter was thick dark yellow. She had fresh skate for Mollie and Dodie.

They arrived and Uncle Craig showed them in. Dodie and Mollie Edgar were given pride of place in the matching armchairs close against the hearth. Archie knelt on the homemade peg-rug between them. Aunty Brenda had built the log fire so high that the flames vanished up the chimney. With five people in the sitting room the place seemed overcrowded. But Archie loved it. He loved having persuaded his parents to come all the way from Aberdeen just to catch sight of his long-eared owl.

They had to eat in the kitchen; it was the only place big enough to accommodate five people sitting. Archie knew it would be Aunty Brenda's fish supper special. He was given the big captain's chair at one end of the table. This was Archie's weekend. He revelled in it.

Mollie asked, "When are we going to see this owl of yours, love?"

Archie looked down the table and caught his uncle's eye: he wasn't sure.

Uncle Craig said, "Early in the morning, I thought. That okay, Little'un?"

Archie beamed, nodded, stuffed a forkful of chips into his mouth.

Aunty Brenda said, "Steady now, it took me a long time to cook those. Don't demolish them all in ten seconds!"

They all laughed as Archie's cheeks bulged. He chewed like crazy.

Dodie Edgar announced between mouthfuls, "I gotta thank you for the job, Craig. It'll be the saving of us, I'm sure."

"Not at all, Dodie."

Archie had forgotten all about it. "Job?" he said. "What job's that, Dad?"

"Watcher."

"What?"

"Watcher for the Forestry Commission." He laughed. "I'll be out in these here forests now, keeping an eye on you and your owls!"

Archie grinned at his parents and his aunt and uncle laughed. He couldn't recall being so happy. He couldn't remember the last time a shared meal had been so light and carefree. It must have been years ago. The Christmas dinner had been utterly miserable.

The early morning was cold, the skies blue for once instead of slatey grey. They all stood back from the garden shed whilst Uncle Craig tapped lightly on its door.

Dodie Edgar whispered, "What you do that for?"

Archie answered, "Password."

His mother said in a hushed voice, "You know all about it, then?"

Uncle Craig, lifting the door latch, turned and told them, "You'd be surprised what Little'un knows. This kinda learnin' disnae happen in a classroom."

The door was opened wide.

Inside, in deep shadow, Free sat quietly on her perch. She didn't seem at all bothered by the strangers. They all craned their heads forward, crowding the threshold. Then the bird started to rock on her perch.

Archie began to get anxious. "Get back, please get back. She'll get scared. Look, she's bating."

Dodie Edgar said, "She's what?"

"Bating," Archie repeated. "Jiggling around, like. Starting up in a panic. If she was loose she'd fly off by now."

Archie's father stifled a laugh. "You been readin' too many o' them library books!"

Archie felt embarrassed. "No, I haven't, Dad. It's common sense."

Mollie Edgar mumbled, "Your father doesn't have too much of that."

Uncle Craig brought the owl out into bright sunlight. They all stared at her. Archie was struck with wonder. He felt he'd never seen anything so beautiful. Every time he set eyes on Free he felt the same way. It was almost painful because he knew that, within a few months, when the new Rosie arrived, he would release her into the forest. That was to be the moment.

He smoothed her multi-coloured wing feathers. He ran a finger down the silk of her tail feathers. He gazed into the mystery of her eyes. It was always the same magic, the same enchantment. He found himself unable to speak; such was the bird's effect on him.

Aunty Brenda stood at the back of the little group. She always liked to blend into the background. But now she smiled. "This is the first time I've seen that creature, and I've heard Craig and Archie do nothing else lately but talk about it. I can see why. She's something to behold."

Mollie Edgar had tears in her eyes.

Archie turned to his mother, wondering why she was so silent. Then he saw the tears. He was baffled. There had been so many tears over the past year – and now there were more. Archie became worried. "Mam?"

Mollie smiled through the tears and nodded as if to say, I'm fine, I'm not unhappy, it's nothing, ignore me. She found a tissue and wiped her eyes. All this time she had been transfixed by the owl as it sat on the gauntlet on Uncle Craig's forearm. She couldn't take her eyes away from it.

Archie said, "What do you think, Mam?"

"She's amazing."

"I told you so."

"I've never been so close to a real owl before. Only seen pictures in books, bits o' film and that."

"Books can't do this, Mam?"

"No, no, nothing in a book's ever brought tears. . ." Mollie Edgar couldn't finish the sentence.

She began to sob openly. Her shoulders shook up and down. Aunty Brenda stepped forward and hugged her sister. "There, there, Moll."

Dodie Edgar stared at his wife in amazement. What on earth had brought this on? She hadn't blubbed like this since Rosie. . . His thought crashed.

But, deep down, without being able to put it into words, Archie knew. Something had changed in his mother's heart. Something massive. And Free had been the trigger. Now, he was sure, things would be different.

When they got home, Mollie went straight into the backroom to rest. She had all sorts of aches and pains from standing too long. But, beyond that, she was still overcome with those strange feelings the long-eared owl had brought on.

Archie went into the sitting room. His father wasn't there. The sofa was oddly empty and the television screen was blank. He couldn't believe it. So many peculiar things were happening. He went through the house calling, "Dad! Dad!" No answer. He became alarmed. His father never went out without telling him.

Archie went into the kitchen. It was empty. No bacon and egg smell. But then he saw a shadow move across the window from outside. The dark wings of a massive bird. No. Clouds suddenly blotting out the sun. It couldn't be just that. No, it couldn't. It wasn't summer.

Seagulls shrieked from the chimney stacks.

Breadcrumbs fluttered down from the sky, like odd bits of snow.

What was going on?

Archie dashed out the back door.

Suddenly he halted, coming across the weird sight of his father standing still and just staring up into the sky. Just staring like a statue.

"Dad, what are you doing?"

At last Dodie Edgar shifted, turned his head, smiled down at his son. He seemed to have grown a foot in height. "I'm cloud watching, son."

"What?"

"Studying clouds."

Archie was stumped. "What for?"

"New job."

Archie was still stumped. "What?"

"Don't keep saying that."

"Why?"

Dodie Edgar laughed. "Oh, it's 'why' now, is it?"

"What?"

Dodie Edgar shook his head and crouched down and put an arm around his son's shoulders. That made Archie feel strange. His father hadn't done that in years. That's what it felt like. It was more like Uncle Craig.

"Archie, lad, let me explain." Dodie Edgar stared up at the sky again. Archie's eyes followed. "My new job's with the Forestry Commission, right?"

"Yes, Dad."

"Well, I've got to study for it, be trained, like."

"Like training an owl?"

Dodie Edgar laughed. "Not exactly like that! I won't be flying around in circles on a long lead!" Archie saw the amusing image and ended up laughing with his father. "No. I need to be able to recognise different types of cloud to become what they call a 'watcher'." He placed his head gently against Archie's and pointed a finger skywards and they both looked along his finger. "See that big tumbling one there?"

"Yeah."

"That's a nimbus. If you get lots together – cumulonimbus – that's bad news."

"Why?"

"Rough weather ahead. Maybe violent storms."

"I thought you got all that from the newspapers, or the TV weather forecasts."

"Not any more, Arch. I've gotta watch wi' ma own eyes, minute by minute, and radio back if necessary. Forget the small screen – I'm in the real world now!"

Archie detected the tone of pride in his father's voice. Times were changing. Minds were changing. He said, "Aren't you watching the Saturday afternoon sport on the box? It'll be on soon."

As Dodie Edgar stood upright he lifted Archie in his arms. They were both that little bit nearer the clouds. "I don't know that I'll bother today, lad. Your mother needs a few things from town. And besides, I thought I might root around in the loft and dust off the fishing rods."

Archie gave his father a searching look. Was he being serious?

When Dodie Edgar ducked into the kitchen, Archie looked up at the nimbus and thought he saw the shape of a baby wrapped in a white shawl.

CHAPTER NINETEEN

We All Have to Learn

This Saturday morning Uncle Craig allowed Archie to do everything. "You're old enough and you've got to learn if you're going to make an outdoor man," he repeated. He didn't only allow him, he encouraged him.

They went to the shed very early after Aunty Brenda's standard breakfast of 'porridge you could lay on with a trowel and cement bricks solid with'. Archie only ever tasted porridge at Hirn Lodge. It was his Saturday treat and warmed the cockles and made Krispies taste like nothing.

Archie opened the shed and clucked his tongue softly and kind of cooed in the special way that showed Free who they were. Owls have only one common predator: humans. Golden eagles were known to take them but not in coastal area forests, only in the Highlands. So you had to be careful and gentle and go through the fixed routine.

Uncle Craig hardly said a word – but he was watching.

Archie slipped the gauntlet on, then looped the leash in his belt, then tied the jesses at the end of the leash to the ring on the owl's leg, then clucked his tongue once and gave a little tug and the owl hopped dutifully onto the gauntlet. Archie always felt a desire to kiss Free on the sheeny feathers of her head, between the delightful ear tufts, but he always resisted the temptation. You had to stick to routine or upset her.

Archie then walked slowly from the shed to the Meadow up the well-worn path. Uncle Craig sloped behind, watching like a hawk himself. He thought his nephew was a natural but daren't say so.

In the clearing's dead centre, Archie unclipped the leash and slowly raised his perch-arm. Free's head revolved one way and then came back. She was doing some watching of her own. Archie was in the grip of her fierce proud amber eyes; she seemed to hypnotise him. He thought back to his mother's tears. Sometimes he felt the same way: something deep down, touched but barely understood.

Uncle Craig whispered, "Now, Little'un. Go on, fly her."

Archie raised his perch-arm and gave a quick flick and the owl's wings opened like something miraculous and she beat her way through the air.

The sky above the ring of pines was empty apart from thin cloud. Archie felt the tin drum of his heart. 'She's free now,' he thought, 'She doesn't need to come back if she doesn't want to.' Underneath all the training she was wild. She'd find her brothers and sisters – his mind flashed back to fine pure white eggs in a ground nest – and she'd never come back.

Archie remembered his panicky words when Uncle Craig had first flown the owl off the leash: 'She won't come back! She's gone, she won't come back!'

Uncle Craig didn't seem concerned. He craned his head and slowly turned through a full circle, his woodsman's eyes narrowed all the time. There was just more or less empty sky, not even the odd soaring seagull.

Archie asked his Uncle, "Do you think she's gone for good this time?"

"No, Little'un."

"How can you be sure, Uncle?"

"She's hungry."

"Didn't you feed her this morning?"

"She hasn't been fed since yesterday."

Archie thought that was cruel. He didn't understand. "Why didn't you feed her?"

"Think about it, Little'un. If she was well fed when you just released her, she'd be gone an age with a full stomach. As it is, she'll be back soon, you see. She'll be expecting some free meals."

"But can't she do her own hunting?"

"Not yet, she's no used to it, is she? Like everyone, she has to learn. We'll gradually cut her meals down until the day you finally let her go, then she'll hunt. She'll have to."

Archie was amazed at his uncle's wisdom. He seemed to know everything that was worthwhile knowing. Archie thought back to what Miss Lewis had said: 'A wise man who might step easily right out of a bible story. One of the three who brought gifts to the new baby'.

'The new baby.' Rosie. She was everywhere in his thoughts. Yet she was the 'old baby'. She had gone over a year ago now in all that snow.

Archie's mind had gone off in a dream when, as if from a great distance, his uncle's voice reached him: "I say, Little'un, get with it! Raise the gauntlet now. *Now*!"

Before Archie knew what was happening, Free had crash landed on his arm, almost missing the gauntlet completely. He hadn't seen her come in. He hadn't heard her cry or the beating of her wings.

"I've got her, Uncle! I've got her!"

The owl pulled her wings in once she had gained proper balance. Then she quickly settled and all was calm.

Uncle Craig was frowning. He didn't usually frown. His face took on the fierceness of the owl. "You weren't watching, Little'un. Whatever were you thinking of?"

Archie couldn't betray his faraway thoughts. "I'm sorry."

"It's okay this time – but you must concentrate. If she thinks you're not going to accept her, then she'll be off again and who knows. . ."

Archie felt tears welling up. The pebbles in his heart rattled together. He couldn't cry. Not like his mother did. You didn't do that. Free would be aware. He didn't want to upset the owl or his uncle.

Uncle Craig must have noticed. He crouched down and put an arm across Archie's shoulders. This time his voice was silk. "We all have to learn, Little'un."

Archie nodded.

Free sat on the gauntlet and rotated her head as if nothing bad had happened. She was back. She was back and she was hungry.

They walked slowly up the path to Hirn Lodge. Uncle Craig told Archie that he had to nip off in the Land Rover, something about

Dodie Edgar's job. Final details. Aunty Brenda would keep him entertained.

Archie sat in the kitchen thinking so many things: Free in the shed, Rosie in the snow, his mother in the backroom, Rory trapped in the tree.

Aunty Brenda brought him a chunk of home-made Dundee cake. He loved the whole almonds on the top, partly because of the flower petal pattern she arranged them in, and partly because she burnt them ever so slightly the way he preferred.

Archie's eyes lit up. "Thanks, Aunty Brenda!"

She pretended to be cross. "I shouldn't be making you so many tasty things, young'un; your mother'll be after me for fattening you up."

"No, she won't – and I'm not fat, am I?"

"Nay. Not yet. Plenty of time, though." She smiled and pinched his cheek. Archie clamped his mouth over the cherry-speckled chunk.

Aunty Brenda said, "Now then, Archie Edgar."

He stopped working his jaws, gulped the half chewed piece down, gave his aunt a quizzical look. Whenever she said 'Now then' it meant serious business.

"Have I done something wrong?"

"No, lad, but there's plenty you can do right."

Puzzled, Archie resorted to his usual, "What?"

"Not 'what' – 'pardon me'."

"Pardon me."

"That's better." Aunty Brenda watched him finger up the crumbs, every last speck. "I mean when that baby comes along in May. You know very well what problems your mother's had since. . ." She didn't need to finish.

"Aye." Images flew into him: Rosie's death-white face, an owl's plumage.

"Well, she'll need help – your help. Your father'll be away doing his new forest job, hopefully. That leaves you, Archie Edgar."

Archie seemed to stare through his empty plate. Thoughtfully he mumbled, "Aye." And then he asked something he'd never asked her before. "Aunty Brenda, why don't *you* have any children?"

She looked away from the table, out through the window to the forest trees. "It's a long and complicated story." Then she brightened up. "But I *do* have a child – you, Archie Edgar! Now I suppose you'll be wanting another half-ton piece of Dundee cake."

His broad smile provided the only answer she needed.

CHAPTER TWENTY

Three Different Heartbeats

This time when Agnie called, Archie didn't make excuses or try to shoo her away.

She took him to the Town Centre where all the big shops were.

On the way he said, "But it's Sunday, Ag, the shops won't be open."

"Where have you been living, Archie Edgar, on the Isle of Skye? They're nearly all open on a Sunday now."

"My Uncle Craig says it's against God's will."

"What? What is?"

"Shops opening on a Sunday. It's the Sabbath."

"The what?"

"The Sabbath, the holy day of the week."

"Well, for most people it's just another shopping day."

"Uncle Craig wouldn't like it."

"Well, he must be cracked."

Archie stopped in his tracks. Agnie walked on a few paces, then halted and turned round. She saw the look of fury on Archie's face. Agnie said, "What did I say wrong, then?"

Archie yelled, "Don't you call my uncle cracked! I'll. . .I'll. . ."

Agnie said, "Okay, okay, I'm sorry. It's just. . ."

"Just what?" He was fuming.

"You're always going on about your Uncle Craig. Anyone would think he was your daddy instead of your uncle."

Archie felt an awful cold sensation inside him. He couldn't reveal to Agnie the truth of what she'd just said. If only she knew. But he covered up, he had to.

"He's what Miss Lewis calls a wise man. Haven't you heard her say that?"

"No."

"Well, there were three in the Christmas story alone."

"They were taking gifts to baby Jesus."

Archie said, "Aye, the new baby." His mind flew to Rosie's face: the old Rosie, the lost Rosie. He'd only seen it once. There had been no expression on her face that he could remember, just eyes, nose, mouth, the palest of hair and the whitest of skin. But her lips were tinged blue and he sensed at the time that there was something wrong.

Agnie was right; the Town Centre was bustling with shoppers. There were loads of confusing shopping streets in Aberdeen, and they all criss-crossed and if you weren't familiar with them you could get as lost as if you were a stranger in a forest.

They went to a bench which was put there for weary shoppers. The big concrete pots nearby didn't have flowers in, they contained only littered soil. And there was so much pavement, so many signs and lights and big words above shop doors. Archie preferred the simplicity of the forest and the open spaces of the sea. You could sort things out there.

Agnie said, "You don't come here much, do you, Archie?"

"How do you know?"

"I can tell."

"How?"

"The way you look at everything."

"Oh."

Agnie had a glint in her eye. She said, "Come on, Arch, let's go." And she jumped up from the bench.

"Go where?"

"Into one of my favourite shops – Nichols."

It was dark inside the shop. It was pulsing with rock music. Teenagers sorted through racks of clothes. Shop assistants dressed in black blouses and black trousers glided about with hangers dripping with clothes. There were counters full of jewellery, make-up, fancy scarves, little leather bags.

Archie's heart turned somersaults. He felt nervous; he felt plunged into an alien world.

When his back was turned for just a few seconds, Agnie was gone.

He pushed through the crowd. The place was packed, mostly young girls. He felt terrible. He thought he must be suffocating. The music was loud enough to make his chest and stomach reverberate like the skin of a drum.

"Ag, Ag, where are you?"

He panicked, felt closed in, shut down. He imagined Free in the garden shed: a wild bird kept in dark captivity.

Suddenly she turned up. She was holding a necklace, but it was all scrunched up in the palm of her hand and he only saw its glint for a second. Then it vanished.

"How much did that cost you?"

Agnie smiled in a strange way. She glanced all around her and slipped the necklace into her pocket.

"Wouldn't you like to know?"

What did she mean? And why the funny little smile?

Agnie said, "Come on, Archie, I'll show you something."

He followed her around the maze of clothes racks to a jewellery stand where necklaces hung like multi-coloured treasure.

Agnie motioned to him with a flat hand: stay back, stay there. Archie stood close to a rack of quilted jackets, almost as if he were hiding. He watched her. He was puzzled.

She picked up half a dozen necklaces, one after the other. She looked up and down the shop, her face all innocence. Shop assistants drifted by. Then, with amazing speed, Agnie slipped a necklace in the big side pocket of her jacket. Smooth as silk.

Archie felt his eyes widen. He went cold. He should have known. He'd been thick and stupid. Of course. The glint in her eye. The hand closed around the first necklace. Her strange reply.

He wanted to run but he didn't. He'd done nothing wrong.

She came over. "See, it's easy, Arch."

He was still in shock. He mumbled, "Agnie Robson. . ."

She laughed. "It's nothing, Archie, just cheap jewellery. Kerry showed me how to do it ages ago. Now *you* know. It's a bit o' fun."

They walked out of the shop.

They went back to the same bench on the concourse. Archie felt something rise up in his stomach like a dark shadow. It darkened his heart and then his brain.

Agnie pulled the necklace from her pocket and dangled it before Archie's eyes and said in a deliberately grave tone of voice, "Treasure!"

Archie couldn't wait to get back to his bedroom; it always felt like the safety of a nest.

As he lay with his head stuffed into a pillow, he was sure he heard his mother's voice, distant, muffled. For once it wasn't the television.

"Archie? Archie, are you up there?"

She never called up the stairs.

There was something wrong.

He scrambled down the stairs two at a time.

"Mam, I'm here, Mam!"

He rushed to the door of the backroom. She must be having the baby early, she must be in agony, she's afraid it'll be too late again. He burst into the room, wondering what he'd find.

But there she was, his mother, sitting in her comfy chair at the foot of the bed, calm as could be.

"Archie, don't come in like that! What on earth's the matter wi' yer?"

"I thought, I thought. . ." His mind was a jumble of horrible images. "You thought I was having a fit, didn't you?" Mollie Edgar smiled sweetly and patted the bed. "Sit there, Archie, I have a few things to say."

He sat. He felt the rhythm of his heart slow. He gazed about the backroom; it looked different: tidy, dusted, and there wasn't a bottle in sight, full or empty. He turned his attention back to his mother.

"Sorry, Mam."

"Sorry? You've nothing to be sorry about. It's me that should be sorry."

Archie was puzzled. "You, Mam? Why you?"

"Oh, the awful way I've been for the past year and a bit."

Archie studied his mother's face. Then he dropped his eyes to the growing bulge of her abdomen. He thought babies were a miracle, human and bird and everything else. How could such things have been organised in the first place?

Mollie Edgar went on: "I just wanted to say that when you showed me your owl at Uncle Craig's, I felt something change in me. Something that was slipping away came back again. I can't explain. . ."

"You don't have to, Mam. Free does the same for me."

Mollie Edgar gave Archie her warmest smile and leaned towards him and clutched his head against her. He thought he heard three different heartbeats.

CHAPTER TWENTY ONE

Red and Grey and Blue

Uncle Craig didn't take Archie straight to the shed to see Free. He went to fetch his shotgun from a little box room at the back of Hirn Lodge. It was where all the coats hung and the wellie boots were lined up. It was a mass of string and old boxes and peculiar bits of metal. Archie had only seen his uncle's shotgun standing upright in its rack. He said he hardly every needed to use it. When Archie asked why, Uncle Craig said, 'I'm all in favour of life and this means death. But there are times. . .' He didn't go on, Archie remembered; he didn't need to.

Uncle Craig broke the gun and looked along both barrels and snapped the gun shut again. He felt his coat pockets for shells. Archie watched him, feeling nervous and uncertain. He wanted to see Free, as he always did, but he knew there were other things to do.

"Owl's hungry, Little'un. Come on, I'll show you the rat-traps, eh?"

"Traps? You mean you don't shoot them?"

Uncle Craig smiled and lifted the shotgun high. "This isn't for rats."

Archie stared at the shotgun, at his uncle, at the garden shed which was so silent and closed. "What *is* it for?"

"You'll see. If you live away from the city you have to do certain things that city people don't understand. Stuck in houses they never will."

So much puzzled Archie; this was just another thing.

They walked down the familiar path towards the Meadow, but this time veered off to the left. They were only a hundred yards from Hirn Lodge. Uncle Craig showed Archie a sharp dip in the land where there was a ruined brick building overgrown with bracken and ivy. It looked sinister.

Uncle Craig saw the look on Archie's face. "Nothing to be afraid of. Plenty of juicy rats down there. Think of it as an owl's supermarket!"

Archie tried to laugh but no sound came out of him. He couldn't take his eyes off that dark hole in the earth that he'd never seen before.

"What is it really, Uncle Craig?"

"An old quarry – at least a bit of one. They used to dig granite out of there for the houses in Aberdeen. Now it's rat paradise."

Uncle Craig slipped down the loose shale on the quarry side. Archie stayed where he was on the brim. His uncle pointed. "Rat-trap there, and one there and another one over there."

"Are they like big mouse traps?"

Uncle Craig laughed aloud. His voice echoed horribly. "Nay! That'd kill 'em. They need to be fresh for the owl. They're called 'humane traps', because they're like boxes which catch 'em alive."

Archie tried the word. "Humane."

"Aye – at first. Then I take 'em to the shed and kill 'em with a single blow and Free gets her dinner!"

Archie felt revolted. And yet he knew it had to be done that way. He'd read Agnie's present – the Owl Handbook – and he knew that they'd only eat fresh kills. Part of him wanted to release Free to do her own killing.

"Are there any in the traps?"

"Nay. Just checking. There'll be some this evening. We won't let the little beauty starve."

Uncle Craig climbed out of the quarry. "Come on, Little'un, there's work to be done."

They walked deeper into Midmar Forest, beyond the clearing, beyond anything Archie had ever known. Uncle Craig nestled the shotgun under one arm, balancing it gently as if it were no more than a stick. Then he stopped and put out a hand and made Archie stop. And he turned to Archie and put a finger to his lips: don't make a sound. They stood like statues.

Archie stared into the pines. They were dense and dark and strange looking. On one particular tree he saw several squirrels, rusty-red coloured.

Uncle Craig whispered, "That's what I'm after."

"Squirrels?"

"Only the red ones."

He lifted the shotgun slowly and closed one eye. Archie felt himself go cold. He froze to the spot. He couldn't believe that his uncle was about to. . .

Bang!

Archie catapulted backwards.

Uncle Craig's shoulder jerked.

A cloud of smoke drifted over their heads.

Archie saw at least three red squirrels fall out of the pine, mixed in with dozens of cones and a scatter of needles.

The silence that came next seemed worst of all. It was only ended when Uncle Craig turned to Archie, the shotgun still smoking, and said, "Sorry, Little'un, but it has to be done."

"Why?"

"Forest management."

"What?" (That favourite word again.)

"Red squirrels have been taking over for a long time, killing the native greys. They've been imported; they don't belong here. We have to do something to restore the balance."

Archie had no answer: a battle between squirrels of different colours. Where was the sense in it? He felt that nature should be left alone. But then he thought back to last spring: Uncle Craig taking an egg from the nest of the long-eared owl, hatching it, rearing the chick, training it, handing it over. That was interfering in nature. Growing carrots is interfering with nature!

The shotgun blast kept repeating in Archie's head. He daren't go anywhere near the slaughtered squirrels. Instead he looked up at the sky above the pine tops. There were birds flying, going about their lives. No explosions, no smoke.

Uncle Craig touched Archie lightly on the back and said, "Come on, Little'un, your Aunty Brenda'll be wondering where we've got to."

It was the first time ever that Archie had felt a little disappointed in his uncle.

Archie caught sight of his mother putting on her heavy topcoat in the hallway. She never said she was going out; she had nowhere to go anyway. She hadn't been out walking on her own for over a year.

He watched with one eye through the crack in the kitchen door. His father wouldn't know because his laughter nearly drowned out the television. What could he see or hear? Archie wanted his father's job to begin as soon as possible. It would get him out of the house; it would make him normal, like the other fathers of St Bride's kids.

Archie slipped on his jacket and followed his mother down the street. Late March and the snow had gone but the bitter cold was far from over.

Mollie Edgar waddled from side to side now; he'd not seen her walk that way since the first Rosie was coming along.

She walked fast, without looking back. Archie stayed fifty yards behind, terrified that she'd turn and see him and bawl him out. She didn't. She crossed the road endless times and turned left, turned right. She went into a shop and came out with a small posy of flowers.

Archie was stumped. He thought his mother must be going mad. He thought she must love someone else, someone secret, a friend like Rory but someone who wasn't trapped in a tree.

She walked and he followed again, ready to jump behind any large enough object. Not once did she look back. If she was doing something bad surely she would look back.

She reached the cemetery and walked through the open gates without a moment's hesitation. Archie hid behind one of the gate piers. He saw his mother tread on the stumps of frozen grass between headstones. He watched as she bent low and dropped the posy on a tiny slab of marble. Her face looked pale and expressionless. She seemed to be scared of touching the marble.

Archie wanted to yell out – but he didn't, he couldn't, he was petrified.

When Mollie Edgar left the cemetery – she was only there a minute or two – Archie approached the gravestone: it said 'Rosie Edgar, Made in Spring, Taken in Winter, R.I.P.'

Archie bent over the bleached marble and eased just one little flower from the posy. It looked like a blue daisy but he wasn't sure. It was the same colour as Rosie's eyes had been.

When he got home he placed the flower in his elasticated notebook and shut the book and pressed the flower tight. It was like a little fragment of love.

CHAPTER TWENTY TWO

A Different Archie

March slipped into April.

Archie kept going to St Bride's Primary. It was a promise to his mother which he honoured. Most of the time in the classroom he day-dreamed about Free. He felt a tight little knot in his chest when he visualised her shut up in the shed, but he knew that during the week Uncle Craig gave her some exercise. He tried not to think of the rats trapped in the quarry and the red squirrels blasted out of pine trees, but he couldn't avoid such thoughts. He could train an owl but he couldn't train his mind to stay away from unpleasant things. Not even Uncle Craig could do that.

After school one day Agnie Robson caught him at the gates.

"Don't go straight home, Arch."

"Why not? I always go straight home."

"You haven't been to the Den for a long time."

"So."

"So – it's only a bit of a longer way round."

Archie gave her a doubtful look. "I don't like it much there."

"Why, because it's not a forest?"

"No, 'course not."

"What are you afraid of, Archie Edgar? Is it the gang?"

Archie laughed. "Your gang don't frighten me!"

"Prove it, then."

"What?"

"Come to the Den."

Archie thought about it. He wanted to go home. He wanted to see how his mother was. He wanted the cosy nest of his bedroom. But he didn't want to be thought a coward or a wimp.

"Okay," he said, "just a few minutes."

As they detoured from St Bride's to St Kilda's, Agnie told him how the gang had been mad because someone had gone into the Den and ripped the tarpaulin back and generally messed things up. Archie felt like smiling but kept a straight face as he walked beside Agnie. How could you mess things up in a place like that? It was a wreck anyway.

Agnie and Archie stepped through the stone arch into the ruined church. They saw Jamie and Rufus in the far corner, where the Den was, pulling the tarpaulin roof tight and holding it down all around the edges with stones. Two girls were there too; they stood and watched.

Agnie waved and called, "I've brought Archie!"

They stepped over the usual mass of broken tiles, stones, mosaics, lumps of timber and birds' feathers, and got to the dark mouth of the Den.

Jamie dropped the huge stone he had lifted. Its crash echoed around the church's broken walls. "Edgar, what are you doing here?"

Rufus added, "You usually rush home to you mammy, don't you?"

The two girls studied Archie and smiled slyly, waiting to see what he might do.

Archie felt a kind of inner strength which he'd never felt before. He used to allow them to tease him, get under his skin, but not anymore. He said, "I've got better things to do."

"Why d'ya come here, then?"

"Agnie asked me."

"She your girlfriend?"

Archie felt anger rise through him like a hot coal, but he let it subside. Only then he said, "No, 'course not. But I bet she's the leader of your gang."

"Why'd you say that?"

"She's the only one wi' any sense."

Jamie and Rufus looked at each other. The two girls lost their smiles. They had never heard Archie Edgar speak in this way. They were all on uncertain ground.

Agnie said nothing, but inwardly she glowed with pride that Archie would not let himself be bullied by the gang. She stood between the two sides. She wished she'd never asked him to go there. She said, "Someone pulled the tarpaulin off the Den, but it wasn't Arch; he wouldn't do that."

Rufus said, "Who cares? We've got it back on."

Jamie changed the subject. "That owl you keep talking about in class, Edgar."

"What of it?"

"Can we see it?"

"No." Archie didn't need to hesitate. The word was like a door slamming.

One of the girls said, "I love owls, they feel so soft."

The other girl said, "You've never even touched one, how would you know?"

"But. . . I've seen plenty on the telly."

"That's not touching one, that's not even real."

"I know, but. . ."

Archie glared at the two girls; both lost their inclination to speak. The gang saw a different Archie Edgar: full of himself, standing tall, too proud to get involved in their silly arguments. Somehow he seemed to hover above them.

Agnie was glad again that she'd persuaded him to detour to the Den. Secretly she was pleased that Rufus and Jamie and the two girls could no longer get the better of him.

Rufus repeated what Jamie had said about seeing the owl.

Archie's reply was exactly the same: a sharp 'No!'

He felt he had power over them; he'd never felt like that before. He said, "Don't know about you, Ag, but I'm off home." And before Agnie could reply, Archie was striding across the awful debris of the church.

They stood and watched him go and no one said a word.

"Can Agnie come with us, Uncle?"

"Who?"

"Agnie Robson. She's in my class at school." He gulped as he said, "She's a friend."

107

Uncle Craig looked doubtful. He didn't want to descend on Aunty Brenda on a Friday night with an extra mouth to feed. "Well. . ."

"Please!" Archie clapped his hands together as if in prayer.

Uncle Craig laughed and pretended to clip Archie around the ear. "Archie Edgar, you're a little devil!"

It was all fixed up.

Except that he drove all the way back to Aberdeen on Saturday morning to fetch Agnie from her house. Her parents kissed her and she went.

She was incredibly excited. She'd never been deep into Midmar Forest before.

Archie led the way to the garden shed. He asked his uncle, "Did you get any rats from that quarry place?"

"Don't worry, Free has had a few slap-up meals since then."

At the mention of rats, Agnie stopped in her tracks. She looked fearfully at the shed door.

Archie laughed. "Come on, Ag, the rats aren't alive! They aren't even there now!"

Uncle Craig lifted the latch and swung the door open wide.

Immediately there came a great fluttering. Agnie pictured flying rats and stepped back as her body tensed. She felt both excited and terrified.

Archie waited for Uncle Craig to go in with the gauntlet and the leash and bring out the owl. But he said, "Go on, then, Little'un, *you* get her. She's your owl."

Agnie waited as Archie emerged into daylight; Free sat calmly on his perch-arm. He tickled the owl on the breast feathers. Her huge golden eyes were so alert. She stared at the three humans. She seemed complete in herself.

Agnie was overcome with wonder, just as Archie had been.

Archie said, "Well, what do you think, Ag?"

"She's. . . she's. . . I don't know. I can't believe I'm so close to a real owl."

Archie held out his arm. Free fluttered her wings, then swivelled her head to gaze back in the shed. "Stroke her, then, Ag, she won't mind."

Uncle Craig stood back in proud silence as the two children drooled over the long-eared owl. It seemed in some magical way to bring them all closer.

They all trod the path to the Meadow and Agnie watched as Archie flew the owl on the leash and then released her and whistled and clucked to show that he could bring her back. Agnie thought that this was far better than the Den. She was so glad that she'd bought Archie the Owl Handbook. It meant a lot.

Uncle Craig dropped Agnie off when they drove back to Aberdeen. When he dropped Archie off at home, they both realised that for once Dodie Edgar was not slumped on the sofa watching Saturday sport.

He was out in the back garden, cloud-watching.

CHAPTER TWENTY THREE

Taking Flight

Archie sat at his desk, trying to listen to Miss Lewis. It wasn't easy. So many other things flew into his mind. He couldn't keep them away. He didn't really want to. His attention drifted here and there. One moment he heard her words, the next he was off in the clouds, the forest, the sea, the hospital, the Town Centre, the Den, Hirn Lodge and the shed.

"I say, Archie Edgar!" It was Miss Lewis's raised voice, rifled at him. He hadn't a clue what she'd said just before that. It must have been a direct question. "Are you awake or asleep?"

Archie stuttered. "Awake, Miss."

"What's the answer, then?"

He heard a general chuckling around the class.

"What was the question, Miss?"

The chuckling exploded into open laughter. Agnie wasn't in sight. Where was she?

Miss Lewis put her hands on her hips and tilted her head a little; her look drilled a hole right through Archie. The pupils were all too familiar with this.

"Never mind the question now, it's too late."

Just then, as if to rescue him, an older child slipped into the classroom and handed Miss Lewis a folded piece of paper. She opened it and read it. She raised her eyebrows. Then she glared at Archie.

"Archie Edgar, you are to go straight to the school office."

"Pardon, Miss?"

"To the school office. Now!"

As Archie left the classroom the giggling still hadn't died down. But he smiled to himself: none of it had really upset him. He told himself he didn't need Agnie or anyone.

The lady in the office told Archie he must go home right away – it was about his mother. His heart flipped; he went cold from head to toe; then he burned. The lady added, "Something about a new baby. Sorry, the message wasn't clear."

When Archie got into the house everything was silent. The television wasn't on. But there *were* voices coming from the sitting room, not recorded TV voices but real human ones. He recognised them. He was relieved to hear the softened tones of his mother and father.

He pushed the door open very slightly and peeped in. The room had been completely cleaned up and the curtains were open for once and a big cube of lovely light flooded the room.

Then he saw his mother. She was half lying, half sitting along the sofa. His father was on his knees beside her. Both were smiling and looking down at a little bundle of knitted white material.

He whispered, "Mam."

Mollie Edgar looked up. "Archie, you're here! Come and see your new sister."

Dodie Edgar shuffled aside to give Archie room.

Archie knelt slowly beside the sofa, a sense of wonder creeping over him. His mother parted the pure white shawl. Archie saw the tiniest face peeking out. It was pink and shrivelled and the eyes were tight shut. He thought of a fledgling. He could hardly believe it was real. He wanted to say something, but nothing would come. It seemed enough just to be there and stare and take it all in.

Dodie Edgar said, "Well, Arch, what do you think?"

"She's. . . she's. . . I don't know." He felt silly, lacking the right words.

His mother helped out. "Beautiful? Is that the word?"

"Yes, Mam, but more than that."

For the rest of that day, Archie couldn't bring himself to leave his new sister's side.

Dodie Edgar suggested that Archie spend a few extra days with his aunt and uncle to let his mother get over the birth. She was very weak and needed sleep and there were tests the doctors wanted to do. Archie had to agree – he always had to – but for the first time ever he didn't want his uncle to drive him away from Aberdeen and into Midmar Forest. So many things were changing.

It seemed strange being at Hirn Lodge on a Wednesday; it wasn't the usual Friday and it didn't feel like one. Aunty Brenda didn't have a fish supper ready – he'd have to wait another two days for that. And half the time his mind was back in Aberdeen.

Uncle Craig sensed that Archie's spirit was elsewhere. He understood. He tried to do things to make up.

"Right, Little'un, I'll take you to Cullerlie Stone Circle, as I've always promised. The stones are amazing."

They were sitting at the kitchen table. Aunty Brenda, as usual, was on her feet pottering around, chipping in occasionally. She said, "It's a lovely drive down there; you cross a number o' beautiful burns."

"Aye, and now it's May the airs a wee bit warmer and you might even pick out a few flowers."

Aunty Brenda stopped her drying of pots and mused, "When I was down in Kent in May-time all those years ago, you should have seen the blossom on the fruit trees. A white carpet right across the landscape. I'll never forget it."

Archie didn't know what she was talking about; he couldn't picture Kent or anywhere south of the border. It was as foreign as China. And anyway, Midmar Forest and this little corner of Scotland suited him down to the ground: the long cold snowy winter made the short summer that much more precious.

Archie spoke up at last. "I'd like to see the stone circle, Uncle Craig, but I'd rather see Free first." (And, he thought, but didn't say it, my new baby sister).

Uncle Craig replied, "Of course! We'll kill two birds with one stone." Aunty Brenda turned and glared at him. "Oops, I shouldn't have said that. Slip of the tongue."

Archie saw the funny side. He wasn't offended. They all ended up laughing together.

For once, the long-eared owl wasn't uppermost in Archie's mind.

Dear Rory,

I'm sorry I havn't written for so long.   Theres been so much going on.   Ive still got my longeared owl, but now Ive got a new sister as well.   Ive only seen her once.   Now is the time.   I feel nervus about so many things.   It could all go wrong, anything could at any time.   When I said this to Ace he said to me thats life.   Well it is isnt it.   A lot goes wrong and a lot goes rite and somehow you've got to balance the to.   Thats how i see it.   Anyway Rory soon youll be releesed from the tree.   i know that becos free will be releesed and my new sister has been born and these things are conected with each other.

i dont need to rite to you anymore.   Things have changed. Anyway when you leve the tree i wont know where to send my letters.   You've been a good frend.   Ive got Agnie Robson now but Ill never forget you.   You lissened all the time.

Rory Im going to do a big thing tomorrow.   Wach me and keep lissening.   One day in the forest we mite bump into each other.   We mite even fly free together.

Love, Archie

Thursday morning there were a few snow flurries, but not many.

Archie looked out the lodge bedroom window; the pines seemed crowded and sky high and still.   He couldn't see the shed from that angle.

At breakfast he said to Uncle Craig, "I want to release Free now."

His uncle stopped chewing a piece of toast and looked up. "Now?"

"Well, after breakfast."

"Okay. Nae problem."

Uncle Craig dabbed at his mouth with a white paper napkin; then he got up.   "Come on, then."   He knew what the moment meant for Archie.

Archie lifted the latch on the shed; its overlapping timbers were speckled with snow. The morning was grey and cold. Uncle Craig stood well back and let Archie do everything. He was almost an expert now.

He pulled on the gauntlet but didn't bother with the leash. Free made a little barking sound in recognition. She opened her wings and practised a few flaps, as if she knew. Wise owl.

Archie felt thrilled by the sight of her burning yellow eyes in the semi-darkness. He always felt so proud of her. Her plumage glowed in the snowy light.

When he brought her out on his perch-arm he thought she might take flight, knowing that there was no leash. But she didn't, she sat as if she were half asleep.

Uncle Craig said, "Do you really want to give her her freedom now?" He felt sad himself, but dared not admit it.

"Yes, it was a promise. The new baby is born and Free must go out into the wild. She *will* survive, won't she?"

"Oh aye. Although we've reared her and fed her and trained her, her natural instincts will take hold pretty soon. I've seen it before. Nae worries."

Archie wanted to be sure she wouldn't die of starvation. He thought of rats scurrying around the old overgrown quarry, a natural larder.

At first he couldn't bring himself to lift his arm.

Uncle Craig said, "You okay, Little'un?" He studied the strange faraway look on Archie's face. Archie took courage.

"Course I am."

He lifted his perch-arm. Free seemed to grip the gauntlet tightly with her talons. She swivelled her head to survey the territory.

Archie flicked his arm upwards. That was the signal. The long-eared owl gave several mighty flaps of her wings, tousling Archie's hair. He was forced to close his eyes.

When he opened them again, Free was nowhere to be seen.

He thought he heard that familiar bark.

He looked into the sky above the pines. It was soft and grey and empty.

CHAPTER TWENTY FOUR

A Previous Life

Uncle Craig drove Archie back to Aberdeen on the Saturday afternoon. He'd been away four days. For the next day and a half Archie didn't leave his mother's side – or the new sister's. He detected a fresh glow in his mother's cheeks, which weren't so sunken. And when she smiled now her eyes lit up from within.

Archie asked his mother, "What are we going to call her?"

"Well, your father and I have been discussing it endlessly and we can't come to any agreement. It's just 'bairn' at the moment."

"I know, Mam, and that doesn't sound right. Everyone has a name."

"Even an owl?"

Archie smiled. "Yes, Mam, even an owl."

"You got any brilliant ideas, Arch?"

He looked thoughtful, then said, "I might have. I want to look in a special little book first."

"Okay. Leave me alone to feed her, eh?"

For once Archie was reluctant to leave the sitting room, but he went.

On Monday he was back at school.

Miss Lewis called for silence and then said, "Okay, class, its News Time to start off the week as usual. Any volunteers to get the ball rolling?"

And, as usual, everyone looked uncertainly at everyone else. It always took a while for the first hand to be raised.

The pupils were amazed when Archie's hand shot high into the air.

Miss Lewis was delighted. "Archie Edgar!"

"Aye, Miss."

The class were dumbfounded, all except Agnie Robson who leaned forwards and whispered, "Archie, you're a wee devil!"

"Go on, then Archie, the floor's yours."

He knew what that meant; she'd said it before.

"Well, Miss, I've got *two* things. . ."

One of the boys mumbled, "Greedy bug. . .", but the boy next to him clapped a hand over his friend's mouth. "Let him speak, Tommy."

Archie paused, but only for a moment; he wouldn't be put off.

"First thing is. . . my new baby sister was born last week."

There were cheers and a few muted whistles until Miss Lewis raised her hands high and then lowered them for quiet. Archie looked sheepish. "Second thing is, I released Free – that's my long-eared owl – the day after."

A girl interrupted. "Why'd you do that, Archie?"

"I always meant to. I promised. An owl is a wild creature and I was only keeping it awhile. I have a new sister now; I don't need an owl. It doesn't mean I'll forget her." He went on, with touching quietness, "I love both of 'em and I'm not ashamed to say it."

Everyone in the classroom went absolutely silent.

When a great dark shadow crossed the window, only Archie seemed aware of it.

The rest of that school day passed with pleasing calmness, as if Archie Edgar's news had cast a kind of spell on everyone.

When Archie got home from school he saw his father carrying the television set out of the sitting room. It was like removing the altar from a church.

"Dad, where are you going with that?"

"Oh, hello Arch. Good day at school?"

It was just like him to answer a question with a question.

Archie pointed. "That. The television, Dad."

Dodie Edgar looked down at it as if he'd no idea where it came from. It bent his arms in half circles. "It's going in the backroom."

"Mam's room?"

"Not any more. Your mammy's gone upstairs where any civilised person rests and sleeps."

"Won't it be cosy?"

"Aye – you, me, yer mammy and the bairn."

"What about the sitting room then, Dad, with no TV in it?"

Dodie Edgar felt himself going red with the effort of manhandling the television; his arms seemed to be lengthening. "Look, Arch, let me get this thing in the backroom before it drags ma hands down to the floor."

Archie laughed, imagining his father emerging from the backroom with apelike arms, swinging and grunting.

Archie thundered up the stairs and into the biggest bedroom. It had been his father's for the past year or more, but more often than not he'd slept on the sofa with the television buzzing. It was hard to remember that room as anything much.

He suddenly came upon his mother feeding the baby.

She looked up, startled. "Archie! You're home!"

"Aye," he said quietly as he stared at the suckling baby. "And you're home too, Mam."

She knew what he meant; she knew he meant much more than that she was just in the house.

Archie sat with his father in the sitting room. It seemed strange without the television. There seemed to be a blank in the corner of the room. It felt uncomfortable, and yet instead of something being taken away, it felt as if something had been added.

"Aren't you going to put your feet up and roar at the comedy programmes anymore, Dad?"

"I start my job as a forest watcher soon, Arch; won't have much time for viewing – except clouds and whatnot. The TV'll sit there in the backroom like an old friend I've outgrown a little. Still watch the odd mindless film, no doubt. Better things in life really, aren't there?"

Archie stared at his father in disbelief. Then he said, "I think you've come home, too."

When Agnie knocked at the door, Archie knew who it was from the special knock. When he opened the door, she was beaming.

"Come out, Arch? Jamie and Roof want to build a new den and they want us to help them. And they promised not to do any animal experiments anymore."

Archie felt good about that; part of him wanted to go. But he'd already promised his father. "Thanks, Ag, but I'm going fishing with ma dad. It's already arranged. I'll come tomorrow."

Agnie didn't show any disappointment, she was still beaming when she said chirpily, "Okay. See you tomorrow maybe, Arch."

As she walked away Archie's eyes followed her down the street; he used to be so relieved to see her go, but these days he felt a little sad.

The drifting clouds above the rooftops drew his attention. As a few gulls wheeled in from the sea, he thought he saw a different bird-shape amongst them; but he knew that his imagination must be working overtime.

He went in and shut the door.

Archie couldn't recall the last time his father had taken him down to the River Dee. It felt like it must have been in a previous life, before the first Rosie.

Father and son stood with rods aloft about twelve feet apart. Dodie Edgar pulled out the line and whipped the rod back behind his head and cast in. Archie watched closely. He did the same. Both floats bobbed on the choppy, criss-crossing currents. Everything smelled fresh, as if the whole earth had been rinsed.

Dodie Edgar called down the bank, "You haven't forgotten, then!"

"No, Dad!"

"I'll wager I catch more than you!"

"No you won't!"

Dodie Edgar threw back his head as he roared with laughter.

Archie's own laughter made him slip down the soft bank. He landed in mud on his bottom. His father's laughter intensified.

"You daft brush! You're supposed to catch the fish wi' your rod, not dive in after them!"

"I'm sorry Dad, I canna control myself!"

"Well, nobody else is going to, certainly not me."

The rest of the day went like that.

Neither of them caught anything; they'd both lost their touch, but it didn't matter. They knew that they weren't really there in the end to catch fish, but to give Mollie and the bairn a rest, and to see what it felt like to be father and son again.

CHAPTER TWENTY FIVE

A Special Name

Mollie Edgar called Archie into the sitting room; she was feeding the two-weeks-old baby.

Archie popped his head around the door. "Mam? Did you call?"

"Aye. Come in. Bairn's full o' milk and fallen asleep. Look at her."

It felt so nice to go into that room without the blue light from the screen flickering and the jarring buzz of voices and music, laughter and sound effects. It seemed transformed into something more human.

Archie leaned across his mother; the baby's face was creased and peaceful. She's already filled out in two weeks.

"Her face is so tiny, Mam, she's more like a doll."

"Aye, but very much a live one."

"What did you want, Mam? Can I get you anything?"

"A name will do."

"What?" (Again that much used word flew into Archie's mind.)

"Remember, you said you'd look in a special book for a name?"

"Oh aye, I'd almost forgotten. But I did look. Haven't you and Dad come up with your own name for her yet?"

"No, it's ridiculous. We can't really decide – except that we both like 'Ruth'. It needs something following it, though, a middle name, or a sort of double-barrelled first name."

Archie broke into a grin. "I've got one!"

"What's that?"

"Asio."

"What?" Mollie Edgar raised her voice. It came as a shock because it didn't sound like a name at all. "How do you spell it?"

"A-S-I-O. Asio."

Mollie Edgar stared doubtfully into Archie's eyes. "Where'd it come from?"

"My Owl Handbook. The Latin name for the long-eared owl is 'asio otus'. Otus means ears," he added proudly.

Mollie Edgar pretended to be scandalised. "You want to give your new sister an owl's name?"

"Only the second bit: 'Ruth-Asio'. It slips off the tongue, Mam. I think it sounds beautiful."

Mollie Edgar looked down at the sleeping child. "Like your sister."

Archie bent low and kissed the baby's forehead. "Aye."

"All right – but we'll see what your father thinks."

Archie jumped in the air. "He'll love it, too!"

The sitting room fell into shadow just for a moment, then daylight flooded it again. It was as if the wings of a huge bird had passed by. It left Archie in a fit of remembrance.

Dodie Edgar scratched his head. "Ruth-Asio?" he repeated, puzzled, after Mollie had told him of Archie's suggestion.

"Aye."

"Where on earth does the 'Asio' bit come from?"

"He says it's the Latin name for an owl."

"Is it now? I'm not sure I can get used to 'Asio'. Sounds like 'Ass'."

As Dodie Edgar came out of the backroom, he caught sight of Archie gallumping down the stairs.

"Arch, what's all this about 'Ruth-Asio'?"

"I got it from my book – at least the second bit."

"Aye, I know, your mother told me."

"Don't you like it, Dad?"

Dodie Edgar looked daggers at Archie, who felt terrible because he knew now that his father thought the long-eared owl's name ridiculous. But then the daggers magically transformed into a smile.

"I think it's great, Archie! 'Ruth-Asio' it'll be; me and your mother agreed to it. You can slide it together as 'Ruthasio'. Stands out as something special."

121

Archie almost leapt over the bannisters. His heart felt like a box of firecrackers. Without thinking he leapt into his father's arms and his father swung him around and Archie's shoes clipped the walls on either side of the hall. It was years since that had happened.

Mollie Edgar, concerned at the commotion, appeared at the top of the stairs with the baby. "Shush, you two noisy kids, I'm trying to get the bairn asleep!"

Archie reminded her. "Not the 'bairn', Mam, its Ruthasio."

She smiled and shook her head. "I don't know that I'll ever get used to such a name. And what'll the neighbours think?"

Dodie Edgar joined in. "Blow the neighbours. If we want to name our daughter after some daft wee bird, that's up to us."

Archie paused for a moment. His thoughts flew skyward. 'Daft wee bird.' He knew his father didn't mean it as an insult; he was joking. He saw the mottled plumage, the fierce amber eyes, the curved gripping talons; he heard the soft little barks; he watched as Free swooped this way and that around the pines and low over the snow-dusted bracken. He saw the satisfied smile on his Uncle Craig's face. He would be grateful forever.

When his mother came down the stairs with Ruthasio tucked into the nest of her arms, Archie leaned over close to the baby's face.

"I think she's a miracle," he said, and the whole house seemed to flutter and soar on bright wings.